Night of the mate

Robbie Sins

Contents

Aibek Pack Hierarchy and Information

Alphas - Top members of the pack. This group includes the Alpha and his sub-alphas (alphas who are just under The Alpha and are the top pack fighters/protectors/guards).

Betas - Second highest members of the pack, they can be fighters or providers (providers hold high-earning jobs in the real world that fill pack coffers).

Gammas - Middle pack members eighteen and up who are not sub-alphas or betas. They most often hold jobs in the real world that help to fill pack coffers.

Deltas - Pack members from thirteen to seventeen. These pack members can begin training for fighting or real-world jobs, depending on their nature.

Epsilons - Pack members from birth to twelve.

Zetas - These pack members are the lowest of the low; convicted of crimes against the pack that don't merit being killed; the "undesirables" of the pack for various reasons. They do not hold real-world jobs. Called the "green" wolves because they do all the farming for the pack.

Mate Brand - When pack members turn 21, they all wake up on the morning of their birthday (following an unnaturally deep sleep) with a mate brand, a very slightly raised, simple black-lined tattoo on the left wrist unique to the wolf and the wolf's Destined One. Only the Alpha and His Howl have their mate brands on their faces, along the outside of their left eye. (See tattoowoo.com and search wolf2 for an example of what Neera and Night's mate brands look like.)

Destined One - The one wolf in the world meant for you; the only other wolf in the world whose mate brand matches yours.

The Alpha - He leads the pack and has total control over every wolf in it. He is the largest wolf in the pack and has the ability to command every wolf with a simple, spoken directive.

The Howl - The Destined One of the the Alpha. When the Alpha finds his Howl, once they have bitten each other (called the Taking of the Blood), they not only forge a connection, but they also have the ability to shift into one wolf, called the Bonded Wolf; this wolf is twice the size of a normal wolf, more ferocious and more deadly than any other single wolf. The only wolf that can successfully fight and defeat a Bonded Wolf is another Bonded Wolf.

The Alpha's Teeth - The pack's enforcer. He does the disciplining in the pack, he carries out the Alpha's commands.

Taking of the Blood - When two Destined Ones bite each other to seal their connection. When this happens, all desire for any others dissipates and an unbreakable emotional connection between them is created where they can feel each other's emotions and sense the other's thoughts.

Alpha Decree - A command from the Alpha that no wolf can resist; a wolf has no choice but to obey an Alpha Decree.

Chapter 1: The Alpha's Howl

He rejected me.

On the morning of my twenty-first birthday, I came awake slowly, feeling different, and I knew it was because my mark had appeared while I had been in an unnaturally deep sleep -- I had been warned that would happen. With my eyes closed, I put my left wrist in front of my face and then slowly, slowly, opened my eyes.

The mark wasn't there.

I shot up in bed, looking frantically at my right wrist, my arms, even my legs. Once, twice, three times I checked all of my limbs.

Nothing. I had no mark.

Since that left only one option -- impossible though it seemed -- my heart began pounding wildly as I raced to the bathroom to look in the mirror.

And there it was, curving along the outside of my left eye. My mate brand.

I sucked in a breath, disbelieving, my fingers gently following the slightly raised lines.

Somewhere between a brand and a tattoo, the mark was permanently etched into my skin. A few simple lines showed a wolf with its head thrown back, his neck dissolving into a few sharp swirls.

It was the Alpha's mark, and everyone knew that mark because the Alpha's mark was the symbol for our pack. The fact that my mark was on my face also pointed to me as the Howl.

I was the Alpha's Howl.

Only the Alpha and his Howl had the mate marks on their faces, leaving no room for anyone to doubt our places in the pack.

He was the Alpha.

I was his Howl.

He was eight years older than I was, and his mark had been there since he had turned twenty-one. His girlfriend's mark did not match his and hers was not on her face, so he knew -- everyone knew -- Lindsay Morgan was not his Destined One. She was not his Howl.

I was. He was mine.

A surge of possessiveness rose up in me, and I felt my wolf snarl, her jaws snapping at the thought of another female with my Destined One.

She was immediately territorial. Restless. Wanting to get to her mate so we could Take the Blood and mate.

After I threw on some shorts and a tank top, I ran barefoot to the Alpha's house, about a mile from my apartment complex. His house was a small log cabin set by the river's curve -- I had the idle thought we would have to build onto it to accommodate all of our children since Alphas were known to be prolific -- and I finally climbed up the steps and knocked on the front door. A minute later Lindsay Morgan opened the door, and I took a step toward her, baring my teeth, not liking the scent of the Alpha -- my Alpha -- all over her.

The color drained from Lindsay's face as she noticed my mark. I'm sure she'd been dreading this day for years, since the very moment they'd become lovers.

It took her a moment to find her voice, and when she did, it was shaky when she called for him, my mate, her as-of-this-moment former boyfriend she'd been with for the last three years. Every pack member thought Night had been foolish to have a girlfriend, especially so serious a one, when she was obviously not his Destined One. Yet he had backed everyone down when they had brought it up to him as an unwise move -- he had boldly declared the two of them to be in love. Again, I felt my lips pull back from my teeth, and Lindsay bared hers in return as the Alpha walked up to us.

Reeking of her.

That was going to end. Maybe an acid bath was in order to remove her nasty stink from my Destined One.

Night stilled when he saw me, saw my face, saw his Destined One in front of him after all these years.

"Night," Lindsay's voice was a soft cry, pleading for something, though I wasn't sure what. But I would.

Night's golden eyes met my green ones, and for a brief moment, energy arced between us, fierce and strong -- until he looked away, breaking the connection.

Brushing past me, he stepped onto his porch and howled, calling all of the pack adults to the Den, our community room, a place for all wolves in the pack to meet, have fun, be with one another.

He looked back at me without looking at my face, and took hold of my upper arm. With his other hand, he snagged Lindsay Morgan's hand -- my arm, her hand -- and walked us toward the Den.

Without saying a word.

Wolves from all over the pack lands were converging on the Den, some in human form, some in wolf form, all of them curious about this rare summons so early on a Saturday morning, no less. Night took both of us to stand by the fireplace.

For one brief, fleeting moment, when he first brought me to the gathering of our pack, I'd had hope. Even though Night had grabbed me painfully by the upper arm on the way over here and had held Lindsay Morgan's hand, I'd held onto a small bit of hope that he was about to announce me as his Howl. What other option was there for him, for us?

But the look on his face scared me. He was not a happy wolf.

Once everyone had gathered, looking at the three of us curiously, before he addressed our pack, his eyes had met mine again. Then I'd jolted with what was happening in that moment: our hearts began beating in sync, our breathing integrated, breath for breath, our mate brands pulsed, and those first furls of connection had just started to form when he snapped himself out of the mate daze as he'd, too, realized what was happening between us. Night had turned away, breaking off what had been our beginning. I started to crumple at the loss, my breathing starting to pick up in panic, knowing now this meeting was not going to end well for me -- but he gripped my arm tighter and forced me upright.

He turned to me and, in a low voice vibrating with hate, gave me two Alpha decrees I could not ignore. "Do not shift. Do not take your eyes off of me."

He must have been afraid I would shift and rip his girlfriend's throat out. And there was only one reason why I'd do that. No. Please, no. Please don't do this to me.

But as I was to learn, it was not fear of that happening as to why he gave me those decrees. It was to teach me a lesson I would never forget.

"Neera Karis appeared at my home this morning, on her twenty-first birthday, with my mate brand on her face."

All eyes turned to me, although they had already noticed that I bore the mark of the Alpha's Howl.

"I find no joy in this one." He pointed at me, his voice scathing and derogatory, and I was unable to look away. "There is nothing within me that feels the pull of the bond, that she is truly my Destined One."

He may as well have been slicing me open with his claws for all of the hurt he was inflicting. Rejecting your Destined One went against everything we were as wolves, and he was lying. I knew he had felt our connection.

Murmurs ran throughout the room as everyone began to realize they were about to witness something so rare, not one person here had witnessed it, although most of them had heard faint rumors of it happening in other packs throughout history. The growing tension was becoming unbearable, and I heard many growls and yips of the wolves as they became uncomfortable with something so unnatural that they had to express their unease.

"So I state here and now, with all of our pack as witnesses, that I reject Neera Karis. I reject her as my Destined One. I reject her as my Howl. I declare my loyalty to Lindsay Morgan, and it is to her that I declare my allegiance and my devotion."

He may as well have reached his hand into my chest and pulled out my heart. My wolf howled, desperately trying to break free but unable to ignore the Alpha decrees.

"Please," I pleaded with him, my voice a mere whisper that I knew he could hear because I was his Howl, no matter what he declared. "Please, I'm begging you, don't do this."

He stroked her face in front of me, while with his other hand, he undid his pants, and pushed them down, his cock huge and hard.

"Please, don't do this." My lips were barely moving, and even if I wasn't being held back by the Alpha's decrees, I don't know if I could have moved.

Lindsay Morgan smiled at me and slowly bent over a chair she had pulled over so she was facing me, and he pushed up her dress, and without warning, he pushed his cock into her and began fucking her, his eyes on me the whole time. And try as I might to fight it, because of his decree, I could not take my eyes off of him as he pounded into her, groaning in pleasure as he fucked her, hard.

We were wolves. Nudity and public sex, rough and raw and wild, were nothing to us. It happened all the time, and no one thought anything of it.

But never, ever had anyone seen sex used to reject a Destined One. And not just any Destined One -- this was the Alpha rejecting his Howl.

Night must have been deadly sure that he had enough strength not to need me. When an Alpha and his Howl mated, when the bond was secured by Taking the Blood, the two would shift to form one wolf, the Bonded Wolf, the size and ferocity of which could be challenged only by another Alpha and Howl Bonded wolf.

He kept his eyes on me the entire time he was fucking her, and even as he came, he would not close his eyes or take them from mine. His eyes burned as he pulled out of her, then turned her around, pressed a violent kiss to her mouth -- still with his eyes on me -- then pushed her down on her knees to clean him off as he watched me watch him. Watch them.

He saw the agony in my eyes. He saw the pain -- he may even have felt it. And he rejoiced in my pain.

Not only was he giving up our Bonded wolf, he was giving up having children. A male wolf could have sex with another female who was not his Destined One, he could even have the sensation of an orgasm, but he had not even one drop of ejaculate. A male wolf only had ejaculate with his Destined One, could only have children with her.

I could have given him everything a wolf wanted, especially an Alpha wolf such as Night. Yet he had just rejected me. My wolf was now howling her agony. And the human part of me? It had crumbled into dust at being rejected publicly. Humiliated publicly.

Forced to watch Night fuck the woman he chose over his Destined One, his Howl.

When he had zipped up his pants, all pack members uncomfortably eyeing Night with wide eyes, he spoke to them again.

"She," again with the derogatory tone as he pointed at me, not even calling me by name, "is now to be the lowest member of the pack and treated as such. She is Zeta."

I was already down, but still he kept kicking. So it wasn't enough what he had done to me. The rejection, the humiliation, the pain of watching my Destined One fuck another -- he was now changing my pack status to lower than the epsilons. Instead of being comfortably in the middle as a gamma, I was now the lowest of all; I was a Zeta. In case I had missed the lesson, he was reinforcing it.

I was now the lowest of the low. I was rejected. I was nothing.

He turned to me, and with a cold look, told me to leave without a word. It was issued as a decree so I couldn't stay and go after Lindsay Morgan as I wanted to. Curled into Night's side with his arm hugging her close, she smiled at me and wiggled her fingers in a mocking goodbye.

I stumbled out of the silent room, all eyes on me, looking down to see if I was actually leaving a trail of blood behind me on the floor or if it just felt that way. No one laughed, no one whispered, no one catcalled, no one howled. They were all stunned, most likely. It was bad enough to hear of someone rejecting his mate, but for the Alpha to do so? Unprecedented. I left in complete silence, my shoulders back, my chin up, needing to retain my dignity despite the way the Alpha had demolished me.

On autopilot, I ran back to my apartment, my wolf refusing to come out. She was beaten, agonized, laying on her side and panting with the pain. I wanted to do the same, but I couldn't. I couldn't lay down and die for my pack members to find me.

I needed to find the Raevyn. The legendary Raevyn Guérir. There were rumors about her, many whispers, and one of them was that, in those rare cases of mate rejection, she could help with the pain of the rejection. She could not sever the connection -- that was impossible -- but she could help with the pain so thinking and functioning was possible. It was gossip, rumors, nothing more. But she was the only chance I had because living with this pain? Unbearable. Living as a Zeta? Unthinkable. Living with having to see my Destined One with Lindsay Morgan? Not possible.

Night would either have to issue a permanent decree that I could not touch Lindsay Morgan or he'd run the risk of me attacking her...and then he would rip my throat out the first time my wolf went after her. By not issuing a permanent decree, he was essentially sentencing me to death.

Even without the Taking of the Blood, no wolf could stand to watch her Destined One with another. It went against our most basic nature.

So on this, my twenty-first birthday, my Destined One, the Alpha of the Aibek Pack, had rejected me, his Howl.

He rejected me.

Chapter 2: It Was Just A Bad Dream

From the moment of my birth, I was a member of the Aibek Pack. Masters of the Moon. First I was an epsilon, then a delta and eventually a gamma. I had no problem being a gamma, being the middle of the pack. My father had been a sub-alpha and my mother a beta; both of them fighters, both of them lost in the Aibek-Lunaire Pack War when I had been in middle school. I had been cared for after that by the pack mothers -- those older females who had already raised their young and had taken on the task of raising the many orphans left from that war.

Night had been just twenty-one then, had just received his mate brand and had assumed his role as Alpha after his father had been brutally tortured and killed, separated from his Howl, who had also been killed, so they could not form their Bonded wolf.

Something had snapped in Night and his brother, Néron, after their parents were killed. The Slaine brothers had been an unstoppable force, rallying the Aibek wolves to press forward, not stopping until a bloody, ugly victory had been won with many carcasses from both sides left in the wake of their unrelenting quest for blood. Night and the Alpha of the

Lunaire pack had hashed out a truce, and the shaky agreement had held in the eight years since. No one trusted it would last, and many were amazed it had lasted for so long. Much of that was due to Night's reputation as a fighter, a brutal warrior who never would back down until he had a pile of throats at his feet.

Today I had discovered that brutality extended to other areas of his life as he had shown all of us. My hands shook as I threw my clothes and toiletries into two duffel bags. Looking around my tiny apartment, I thanked the Great Wolves that Night had not issued an Alpha Decree keeping me on pack lands. I'm sure it never occurred to him that I'd leave. I was -- had been -- a gamma. We were rule followers, helpers, contributors; we loved our pack and our positions in it. Night wouldn't think I'd be bold enough to leave.

And that was why I needed to leave, fast, before he thought to issue a decree forcing me to stay. I might be broken, I might be in excruciating pain, but I refused to die. I'd text my friends once I left, hoping they weren't already headed over to my place to bring much-needed comfort. They'd try to talk me out of leaving, but there was no way I could remain. Staying here would lead to my death.

On my way out, I grabbed the soft, cashmere afghan my mother had made -- the only real keepsake I had of her besides a few pictures I managed to save of her and my dad.

When I got to my car, I stopped cold. My friends Owena and Echo stood by my old, but reliable, Monte Carlo, duffel bags in hand.

"We figured you'd be taking off," Echo said, pushing her sunglasses up on her head.

Owena nodded. "I'd be running from the law after that clusterfuck we all just witnessed because I would have killed both of those assholes." My friend since elementary school, Owena sometimes lacked a filter.

"Yeah, well, you couldn't have because Alpha Decree," I reminded her.

"So, where are we going?" Echo asked.

"We're not going anywhere," I told them. "I'm going to hunt for the Raevyn, see if she can help me, and you two are staying here."

"Nope," Echo contradicted me. "We're going with you. What kind of best friends would we be if we let you take off alone, no pack to comfort you, have your back? You don't even know what's going to happen to you since he...after the Alpha...now that he's..."

"Rejected me," I finished her sentence firmly. "I can't pretty it up, Echo. My Destined One rejected me and as much as it hurts, I have to face it."

"Well, we'll be facing it with you, then," Owena said. "Now, let me drive us out of here, past the guards. They've seen me driving your car all the time, so they won't ask any questions."

Echo and I hid down in the back, hoping the guards would attribute our scents in the vehicle to the fact that we all drove around in my car all the time. Maybe they hadn't heard about my humiliation in the Den yet and wouldn't be on the lookout for one broken and battered wolf leaving pack lands.

In the end, getting off pack lands was anti-climactic. The guards saw Owena driving my car and waved her on through the gates.

No questions.

No comments.

And then we were free. As soon as were twenty miles beyond pack lands, Echo and I popped up in the back seat, figuring the odds of the three of us being spotted by anyone in the pack on a Saturday this far from pack lands was minimal. Although we may have to go to the city or nearby towns to work during the week, on weekends, we wolves stayed near our pack, close to home.

"So, this is really happening," Echo said, more to herself than to either of us. "Road trip!"

I could barely smile, still reeling from the reality of what Night had done to me.

Echo reached into her duffel bag and pulled out her computer. "Listen, we have no clue what's going to happen to you, to your wolf, as a result of this...this...this..."

"Rejection!" I snapped at her. "If I can say it, you can. I don't want either of you walking on eggshells around me. We all lost our parents in the war, so this can't be any worse."

That was a huge lie. Losing your Destined One could destroy a wolf in days, the will to live just gone. My wolf hadn't made a peep since that fun scene this morning. She was deep in me, not even licking her wounds yet because she couldn't summon the energy. She'd always admired the Alpha -- as a female, it was inevitable -- he was a big, big wolf, his solid black fur thick and soft, his golden eyes watchful of his pack members. Up until today, Night had been a caring Alpha, always concerned with his pack's well-being. Today was the first day he'd ever shown deliberate cruelty to any of us. Lucky me!

Echo researched possible symptoms I could experience from being reject-ed, but refused to tell me any of them.

"No. It's like when you hear about lice and your head starts itching," she said when I demanded she tell me. "I could tell you that your canines growing longer was a symptom and you'd start feeling them with your tongue."

Which was exactly what I was doing at that very moment. Just in case.

"So, I'll tell Owena and she and I'll watch you closely for any of these symptoms. And if we see you exhibiting a symptom, then, and only then, will we tell you the symptom. But right now, we're going to hope for the best and maybe we'll find the Raevyn before you have any symptoms."

I thunked my head against the back of the seat and groaned. "How are we going to find her? Finding her is going to be like finding a needle in a haystack. Impossible."

"No!" Owena smacked her palm against the steering wheel. "We are not going to fail in our mission. We are Aibek pack and we are fighters. No mission is beyond us. We're going to find her and we're going to get you help and it's all going to be good. It's all going to be good."

Buoyed by Owena's optimism, we all settled into our seats for the drive to wherever we were led. Echo researched all the Raevyn legends and stories, reading them out loud to us to see if any of us could pick up a clue. We couldn't, no matter how hard we tried. Raevyn was a mystery and it looked as if she would remain one.

We drove all day and well into the night, stopping for gas and food twice, before we finally pulled into a hotel for some much-needed sleep. Stumbling into our hotel room, we had just enough energy to kick off our shoes before we fell onto the king-sized bed, passing out immediately.

Emotional pain will do that to you.

It will also wake you up screaming from a nightmare.

Echo and Owena immediately shot up in bed next to me, Owena demanding to know what was wrong, Echo rubbing my back and assuring me in soft, sweet tones that I was OK.

"He was...he was..." I tried to catch my breath and willed my pounding heart to resume a normal beat. "He was cutting off my mate brand. From my face. He was trying to cut my mate brand off my face with a knife."

We all absorbed that horror for a moment, and shivered as one at the mere thought.

Owena and Echo exchanged a glance.

"That's a symptom, isn't it?" I demanded. "Bad dreams."

Echo nodded, but never paused in rubbing my back. "It's one of the earliest ones, so that's good. It means it's just starting. We have time."

"And when does the pain start? Like the real pain, not just the I'm-shattered-because-of-what-you-made-me-witness-and-what-you-said pain."

"No," Owena said firmly. "One hour at a time. No worrying about when some old stories said it may or may not happen. You just had a bad dream. That's it. Now, we're going to go back to sleep, get a few more hours of rest, and then wake up ready to drive on tomorrow, wherever we're led."

"South," I said suddenly. "We've been traveling west, but tomorrow we need to go south."

Why I said that, I'll never know.

But we headed south the next day, stopping whenever we needed gas or food. I didn't tell them that the pain had started, a crushing pain that made it hurt to breathe. It wasn't constant, but it came in waves and it was all I could do to hide my body's reaction to the agony.

When we stopped for the night at another hotel, I looked forward to sleeping and maybe escaping the pain.

But once again, after about three hours of a restless sleep, I woke up screaming. Same dream, except this time Night was trying to use a hatchet to remove my mate brand.

Sweaty and shaking, I realized this dream had been worse, more vivid, more intense, and my hand flew to my mark to make sure it was still there. The dream had felt very real.

"You're OK," Echo assured me as she rubbed my back. "You're OK, Neera. It was just a bad dream."

Owena clapped her hands together. "We need to run," she said. "This hotel backs up to a huge wooded area and just beyond it is a river. Let's let the fur girls out and have some fun. They've been cooped up for almost three days, and they need to stretch their legs. Come on. We have a couple of hours before sunrise, so let's do it."

"Sounds good to me," I murmured. Anything sounded better than going back to sleep, maybe seeing Night coming at me with another hatchet or something even worse this time.

We walked out of the hotel and into the woods a little ways before we shedded our clothes and tucked them safely into the low vee of an oak tree.

Then we shifted and my fur girl, a smallish black-furred wolf with green eyes, sprinted through the woods, Owena's and Echo's fur girls following.

We ran and ran, playfully nipping at one another as we splashed in the river and chased rabbits -- but not in a serious way -- until we eventually turned back as the sun began peeping over the horizon, orange and pink and breathtaking.

As we came around the bend in the river, a woman sat on the biggest, flattest rock in the outcropping, watching us. She seemed young, her skin beautiful and unlined. What you couldn't help but notice was her lack of hair and the tattoos that covered her head in a spiral pattern.

And then, because she'd surprised us and we'd been focused on her, we noticed the ravens surrounded her, sitting beside her on the rock, one perched on her shoulder, several circling above her in the air.

She looked steadily at my wolf and smiled. "So, Neera, I understand you've been looking for me and have need of my services."

Holy shit. It looked like the Raevyn had found us.

Chapter 3: My Magical Broomstick

"Raevyn," I breathed out the second I shifted.

She seemed to float down the rocks to us, three naked young women utterly awed by meeting the Raevyn Guérir.

"Let's find your clothes and get back to your hotel so we can move along," she said, her voice low and soft. She flipped her golden blonde hair over her shoulder and walked ahead of us, as if she knew exactly where we'd stashed our clothes.

"Wait a minute," I whispered to Owena and Echo, my voice little more than a quiet exhalation of breath. "Tell me I'm not hallucinating, but wasn't she completely bald a minute ago?"

"Bald as a bowling ball," she laughed. And that was it. No explanation for her hair, no explanation for her being able to hear me. Unless she was wolf, but never had the rumors said that about her.

In fact, Raevyn Guérir may have been a legend, but as we'd discovered on our road trip, she was a very mysterious legend since nothing was actually known about her. The three of us probably knew more about her than any other living creature.

She had a bald, tattooed head. Sometimes.

She also had waist-length golden blonde hair. Sometimes.

She looked ageless. I couldn't even begin to guess how old she was.

She knew things. How to find us. (How did she even know we were looking for her?) Where we'd stashed our clothes.

Once we made it to the tree, we grabbed our clothes and pulled them on, and she continued on to the hotel, through the lobby and up to our room.

"Get packed and let's go. We have things to do," she said. So we threw our dirty clothes and toiletries into the duffel bags and left the hotel, still so early that most people weren't awake yet.

We threw our duffels in the trunk. Echo was driving this morning, and Owena looked at Raevyn. "Are you driving with us? Or...?"

"Or flying around on my magical broomstick? No, it's over forty thousand miles so it's in the shop getting a new transmission." She rolled her eyes at all of us, then got into the front passenger seat.

Owena and I exchanged a glance and got into the back seat. All righty then.

We drove for a while in silence, and then Echo announced she was stopping at McDonald's for breakfast and coffee. She shot a look at Raevyn.

"So, do you...eat?"

At that, Raevyn burst into laughter. "What the hell do you think we are? Some sort of vampire that survives on blood?"

Once again, Owena and I exchanged a glance. "Well," I started to say, "we aren't really sure what to make of you."

With a shrug, she conceded the point. "Fair enough. We'll talk after breakfast on the way to our place."

"Oh," I said as we inched along in the drive-thru line, "do you live with someone?"

"Yes, with me," the bald woman said. Not going to lie, we all lost our shit and screamed.

After we calmed down, the bald woman laughed. "God, that never gets old."

"OK this is...different," I said, trying to be diplomatic and not piss off this woman who had extraordinary abilities that I couldn't even begin to comprehend.

"I can see where you would think that," she agreed.

When it was our turn, we all ordered breakfast sandwiches and hot coffee. We parked and ate our food, then the bald woman directed us back on the highway. "We're just about two hours away, so we have time for your questions."

"I have about a million," I said. "First is, who are you?"

"I'm Raevyn," she said as if that was the most obvious fact in the world.

"Wait, I thought the other -- the blonde lady -- was Raevyn."

"No, I am," she assured us. "My friend is Blaisall." She turned and looked at me. "You two have much in common. Four hundred years ago, she was the first rejected mate."

For a minute, we all just absorbed that shocking-on-so-many-levels information.

"I don't...I don't even know what to do with that," I admitted after a full five minutes of silence.

"It's simple, really. Her mate rejected her. We never knew why, exactly. But he was weak in his mind; his elevator didn't go all the way to the top floor, if you know what I mean. The Forces usually don't give a wolf like that a mate. But in their wisdom, which we can never hope to understand, they did, and he ran off after her mate brand appeared -- and he was never seen again. She was devastated."

"I understand," I said softly. Because I did. The pain had been battering me again today, still not constant, but it was hitting me more often than it did yesterday. "So, you're telling me that Night is weak in the mind and that's why he rejected me?"

"Oh, no," she said. "Alphas since the beginning of time have been strong minded. The Forces never make a mistake with Alphas. No, your mate's mind is well and good."

"I see," I said. So Night had rejected me just because...he wanted to reject me. Because of that bitch Lindsay Morgan. Or maybe because of me. Maybe it was just me.

"The why is not important right now," Raevyn said to me. "We must first deal with the pain, which I suspect is bit worse than yesterday, isn't it?"

I bit my lip as a new wave washed over me with perfect timing. "Yes. It's a little worse," I confessed when I could speak again.

Owena lightly slapped my arm with the back of her hand. "You were supposed to tell us if the pain started!"

"Well, excuse me for not wanting to worry you!" I snapped at her. "I was worried we wouldn't be able to find the Raevyn, and then that would have made you and Echo even more upset, and then I would have gotten upset because you two were upset -- it would have been a mess!"

Poking a finger at my face, she snarled at me. Or her wolf did. "You tell us everything," she demanded. "No more secrets! We can't help you if we don't know what's going on."

I'd never seen Owena lose her temper with me before, but this girl was about to skin me alive, and I could only be thankful she didn't have a knife.

"I promise," I said, chastened. My two best friends had left pack lands with me, and although three was better than one alone, we needed our bigger pack and the comfort and familiarity they provided. My friends had sacrificed a lot to be with me, and I needed to remember that they were there to provide comfort, not to have me play the martyr and protect them from what I was going through.

"You damn well better," Owena grumbled.

"You better," Echo...echoed.

"Raevyn, I still want to know how you and Blaisall...work," I finished weakly, not knowing how to describe what I wanted to say.

"It's a miserable story," she said softly. "Way back when, I was an enchantress in a world filled with many of my kind. Then the wolves and the magicks went to war -- the wolves started it, by the way. They feared our power. They hunted us ruthlessly, using some magicks they'd captured and tortured to get past our spells. The wolves captured me, and held me powerless with one of our captured magicks. I noticed Blaisall standing there, at the edge of the crowd gathered to watch another dirty magick be destroyed, her eyes agonized from the pain of her rejection. They were about to tear my throat out and at the last moment, just as the Alpha lunged for me, I slid out of my body into Blaisall's. I watched through her eyes as my throat was torn out and my body crumpled to the ground."

We all sat silent after that horrifying picture she'd painted, imagining what it would be like to watch our own throats being torn out, spectators to our own demise. We hadn't even realized there were enchanters at one time, so long had it been since they existed in our world.

"I was one of the last magicks alive. The wolves decimated our kind. Maybe a few survived, but if they did, they hid themselves well and cloaked their abilities so they could survive. In all these years, I have not heard of another one, but I have to believe that more than I survived. The funny thing is, in their pursuit of destroying us, by killing off the magicks, the wolves lost their longevity somehow and began dying off after living a hundred years or so. We magicks were the fountain of youth for all magical creatures, apparently."

"I'm so sorry," I told her, and Echo and Owena murmured their agreement. "We definitely weren't taught about that war in school."

"That was a dark time in the history of the wolves, a shameful time that I do not doubt they wish to forget. Back then, they tore out our throats with joy, but many generations later, the memories of the war had faded, the reality of the magicks was gone for the most part -- and like many things in history, it became a story and then it faded away."

"So, ummm, you don't have a vendetta against wolves or anything, do you?" Owena asked.

Raevyn gave a short laugh. "I live in close quarters with one, you could say, and that would make things quite uncomfortable."

"So how does it work?" I asked. "Sharing a body, I mean."

She shrugged. "Give and take. Sometimes she wants to be out -- if we go in public, Blaisall is always out and moves me aside. Other times, I move her aside when I want to be out; but sometimes when she is out, I simply watch through her eyes. I am stronger than she is with my magic and I could control her, but we find it works better if I don't. It's unfair."

"And what about her wolf?" Echo asked.

"She is there, and occasionally she gets a run, but since the rejection, she is mostly quiet. I help with the pain of the rejection in exchange for my life."

"Blaisall still feels it?" I asked, terrified, trying to imagine hundreds of years of feeling even worse than I was already feeling.

"Indeed, she does," Raevyn said. "Being rejected by your Destined One is a pain like no other."

"Great," I said.

"I can help, Neera. Since Blaisall, I have helped the four others who were rejected."

"So I'm only the sixth one to be rejected?"

"Yes," Raevyn said. "But the first Howl ever. That is simply unprecedented, and I have never heard the like in all my years. No Alpha would ever reject his Howl. That is giving up a power like no other. Until now, it has been unthinkable. Rejecting the Howl sent by the Forces is just...not done."

Wanting to turn the subject from me being a Destined One loser like no one before me in the history of wolves, I asked, "Can you sever the connection?"

I was hopeful that maybe the rumors were wrong.

"Absolutely not," she stated firmly, without hesitation. "But I can help you with the pain. Relieve some of the discomfort so you can lead a somewhat normal life. I don't say this to discourage you, but you will always have pain. I can make it bearable, nothing more."

"That's better than nothing," I said, feeling a bit dispirited.

"It is," Raevyn said with a decisive nod. "You're already finding the pain uncomfortable, and it only gets worse unless I help. Be thankful there were others before you -- I learned a great deal through trial and error."

"Do you have to take over my body, too?"

She actually laughed at me. "No, Neera. I don't."

"So how do you do it?"

"Some spells. Some potions."

Echo jumped into the conversation. "How did you find us? I've been trying to figure that out."

"A rejected mate is big news," Raevyn said. "Almost immediately, we heard whispers and rumors that the Alpha of the Aibek Pack rejected his Destined One, his Howl. Brutally rejected her in a manner so terrible --"

"OK, OK, we've already read the book and know how that story ends. We don't need to keep revisiting it," I grumbled.

"You'll need to take the next exit," Raevyn directed Echo. "We're almost to our home. Anyway, Echo, to answer your question, I called her to me. It's a lovely little bit of magic that guides the one in need to you."

"That makes sense," I said. "Because I was freaking out trying to figure out how in the heck we were going to find a mysterious legend that might not even exist."

"Oh, I exist," Raevyn said breezily.

"Just one more thing I want to know," I told her. "Am I the only one feeling the rejection, or does Night feel it, too?"

Raevyn smiled. "Now that's a very good question."

Chapter 4: It Was A Blur To Me

"Alpha," two of the females in my pack nodded to me as my brother, my enforcer and I walked toward the pack offices. Strangely, they moved right past me without smiles, not even attempting to stop.

They were not the first ones this morning who had been...distant to me. This was beyond unusual behavior since my pack members always stopped to take my hand for a moment. My Alpha's touch was soothing, comforting to my wolves and I touched hundreds of hands a day.

"They're not happy with you," Aymeric said in a voice so low only my brother and I could hear him. As my enforcer, as the Alpha's Teeth, Aymeric made it his business to know what was happening in the pack, what the mood was, what rumors and gossip were swirling around.

"You completely upset the pack when you rejected your Howl," he continued, "if for no other reason than to provide further protection for the pack. The Lunaire pack Alpha doesn't have his Howl -- yet -- so you having yours would have been an advantage for us and a deterrent to the Lunaires if they thought of trying to break the truce. They do not like that you rejected what could have been so advantageous to us."

"It's more than that," Néron sneered at my enforcer. My brother had been the one most obviously upset at what I'd done, or at least the only one bold enough to get in my face about it. Being my only sibling had both advantages and disadvantages, but one of the advantages was that he spoke quite freely to me, as no other member of my pack would dare.

"You took years of tradition and threw it aside. You rejected your Destined One, your motherfucking Howl, Night -- sent by the Forces -- and you did so without hesitation. There have been rejected mates before, not many, but a handful. But you're the very first Alpha to ever reject his Howl. I don't understand it. Nobody understands it. OK, so you have feelings for Lindsay Morgan, but you shouldn't have been able to resist your Destined One. Your feelings for Lindsay should have faded away to nothing the moment you faced your Howl. From the moment you were born, Neera was stitched into every fiber of your being...and you resisted that. Hell, you not only resisted her, you rejected her."

For a moment, I remembered looking into her eyes. Neera's green eyes, so bright when she stood on my porch, looking at me, her mate brand visible. For just a minute, I felt the invisible bonds between us forming until, for some reason, I looked away. And then I'd decided to call the wolves to the D en.

"Well, now word's out about what happened. It spread like wildfire, Night. I can't even tell you how many calls I've fielded from other packs -- from Australia, China, Saudi Arabia, Brazil, Canada, to name a few -- all wanting to know what sort of fuckery was happening that you could reject your Howl."

My brother glared at me, then continued. "The rejection was on one level, but then you changing her pack status? What the fuck was that? You hadn't already humiliated the poor girl enough by fucking Lindsay right in front of her and telling everyone assembled that you didn't want your Howl?"

The whole time in the Den? It was a blur to me, a vague fogginess that was not clear in my mind, as if --

"She didn't show up with the other greens today," Aymeric said, trying to interrupt my brother's tirade.

I'd been rubbing my chest as he spoke, but the pain that had begun wasn't going away. "Well, did you fucking check on her?"

"Sent one of my men," Aymeric confirmed. "They said she wasn't at her apartment. Her car wasn't there."

"Maybe she'd gone into town to give her notice?" Néron suggested.

I rubbed my chest, the pain still squeezing my insides. "That seems likely. Neera has always been dependable. She wouldn't want to just leave her job without telling her boss."

Néron looked at me as if I was stupid. "She would have had to tell Aymeric, asked his permission, if she was planning to do that. Zetas aren't allowed to make a move unless it's cleared through Aymeric first."

"She might not have known the new rules."

"Oh, come on, Night. Be real. Every pack member knows. Every last one knows how things work with the zetas."

The pain in my chest only seemed to intensify. "Then maybe she just went for a run today because she was pissed."

"Again, not reporting for duty would have to be cleared through Aymeric."

"I hope nobody got to her," Aymeric said in his quiet way. "It seems unlikely with our safeguards, but you left her swinging out there alone, Alpha. A Howl is valuable, even one who hasn't Taken the Blood. Our enemies could take her to prevent you from ever changing your mind."

"So if she's not here and her car is gone, it's obvious she went into work."
Stupid chest pain.

"We called the business. She phoned in sick and said she was ill and needed to take an emergency leave of absence. For an indefinite amount of time."

"Then the obvious answer is she's out for a run, without permission, and one of her friends took her car for the day." That had to be it because anything else was unthinkable.

Néron and Aymeric exchanged glances. "Her two good friends are also gone. I checked back with all of the guards for the last twenty-four hours. One said Neera's car went through the gate at 9:37 a.m. yesterday. She wasn't in the car, however."

"Did they stop and search the car? To be sure? Or are they just talking out of their furry asses?" I demanded.

"No, Alpha," Aymeric said evenly. "There was no reason to stop the car since there had been no orders issued to search vehicles yesterday."

"You also didn't issue an Alpha directive for her to stay on pack lands," Néron reminded me. "Leaving the way clear for Neera to run away from the hell you set up for her when you made her a zeta."

Fucking little brother. Always such a pain in the ass.

"So where is she?"

"Unknown," Aymeric said. "The three of them are not answering their phones."

"What are you doing to find her?" Shouldn't this chest pain stop soon?

I could feel my voice changing as my wolf pushed forward. He didn't like this, didn't like what had happened yesterday. I didn't either, and I wish I could remember why I had --

"The fuck you care?" Néron snapped at me. "You rejected her -- brutally -- you changed her pack status, you didn't order her protection, so you were just about begging for something to happen to her. Now you and your non-Destined One can live happily ever after without all those children you clearly don't want to have and throw the pack into further chaos when you die and there's no successor to take your place."

"Watch yourself," I growled at him, feeling myself on the edge of a change. He might be my brother, but he still had to respect me as Alpha. My wolf demanded it.

"Someone has to make you see what you've done! You've practically alien-ated the entire pack, Night! You took something sacred to all of us and made it into something horrifying and humiliating. You might as well have torn that poor girl's throat out because you absolutely gutted her. So you tell me, what the fuck did you expect to happen? You didn't issue an Alpha decree that she could never touch Lindsay, so you know how that was going to go. Your Destined One couldn't stand by and watch you with another female -- it was only a matter of time before she attacked Lindsay Morgan and then you'd kill Neera in retaliation. So what sane, clear-thinking person would stay on pack lands just biding her time before she brought about her own death?

"I can't explain it!" I shouted at him. "Something happened!" I bellowed, and then I forced myself to calm down and pushed back my wolf.

"Something happened," I repeated, this time more quietly.

"What happened?

"I don't know, Aymeric. It happened twice. Once to a lesser extent when I was at my house and Neera was on my porch. I looked into her eyes and felt the bond start. Then I stopped looking at her, and the connection was broken. It was like --"

"What, Alpha?"

"It was like somebody turned my face to make me stop looking at her."

"Was it Lindsay?"

"No, Néron. She didn't lay a hand on me. Then I was calling everyone to the Den and I grabbed Neera's arm and I grabbed Lindsay's hand. We walked over to the Den and stood in front of the fireplace."

I remembered looking into Neera's eyes again, this time long enough for our hearts to beat in sync, our breathing to match breath for breath, inhale for inhale, exhale for exhale. My mate brand began to pulse and those links of connection had just started to form when I -- I don't know what. I'd felt a surge of power move into my body, pushing my wolf down even as he fought against it, and I was...shoved aside, turned away from Neera, breaking off what had felt so much like the beginning of a powerful bond, even without the Taking of the Blood.

The rest was like trying to see yourself in a fogged-up mirror after a shower. Vague impressions. My memories were incomplete bits and pieces. I could remember a few distant, disjointed words here and there, some incomplete phrases, but it was like hearing something underwater.

Then Neera walking away. Less fuzzy.

Neera walking out the Den doors. That was a bit more clear.

I felt the eyes of my pack members on me, slack jawed, eyes wide, silent.

Shocked.

I looked out at them, and their heads dropped in shame.

Shame at something I had just done. Shame at something I had just said.

Disapproving.

But what exactly had I done? What exactly had I said? It was just at the edges of my consciousness but I couldn't pull it up. I felt...off. My wolf was practically comatose, as if he'd been knocked out and was down for the count. I couldn't rouse him, and it would be several hours before he would come back. Wobbly. Confused. Dazed.

Join the club.

At that moment, before I could wrap my head around what had just gone down, I felt power leave me and I staggered, just as Lindsay Morgan gasped and then crumpled to the ground.

Very clear.

Not a minute later, I followed her.

When I came to, Néron, Aymeric and the pack doctor were leaning over me.

"Alpha," the doctor said. "Welcome back."

Then he walked me through a series of questions that I was able to answer more and more readily as the fog lifted. I sat up after a moment, feeling for my wolf, but he was groggy, too, whining softly.

"You scared the fuck out of me," Néron said, and he looked a bit gray. I was on a couch in the Den, and Aymeric offered me a glass of water that one of the zetas had brought to him.

"What time is it? How long was I out?"

"Hours," the doctor said. "Almost three hours, Alpha. "I've never seen the like before in all my years."

"And Neera?" I asked, remembering her standing in front of the fireplace with me.

The three men exchanged concerned glances.

"What?" I demanded.

"What do you want to know about Neera?" Aymeric asked.

"Where is she?"

"What do you remember," my brother asked, his face pinched.

"The last thing I remember clearly is her being on my front porch, maybe a little bit when she was in front of the fireplace with me. So, I'll ask again, where is she?"

"Alpha, I need to examine you again. Maybe you hit your head harder than we thought. Although after three hours, you should be completely healed no matter how hard you hit it."

Angry, frustrated, I brushed his hands away. "Where is Neera?"

"Night," my brother said, impatience and disgust in his words, "you reject-ed her. In front of the entire pack. Are you telling me you don't remember fucking Lindsay Morgan right in front of her and then demoting her to zeta?"

No. No, I did not.

All I could say when they related the events of the rejection to me was I couldn't remember it clearly. My wolf was whining for Neera, but my brother and Aymeric told me I needed to give her some time.

I didn't want to.

But I was still weak, and I didn't like that at all. Not one day in my life had I been weakened like this. I had Alpha strength and power, but I felt like my body had been hit by a truck.

"I want you to stay with me for a few days," Néron said. I agreed, even when Lindsay Morgan -- who had been carried back to my house after she had fainted -- had come bursting into the Den, demanding to see me.

The doctor had turned her away.

I hadn't seen Lindsay for more than a day, but my focus was Neera and I was now trying to absorb the fact that she'd pulled a runner. Not that I blamed her after what I had done to her in front of the whole pack. From all accounts it had been brutal, and that I had done that to my Howl was fucking with me and pissing off my wolf.

My brother and Aymeric hovered around me for the next two weeks, refusing to let Lindsay see me, worried that my wolf might kill her as the cause of being without our Destined One. She screamed and demanded and cried, but Néron and Aymeric stood firm. With each day that I was away from Lindsay Morgan, I felt a clarity I hadn't felt in three years returning.

But a week after the rejection, I began to have vivid nightmares about Neera, where she was trying to cut off the mate brand on my face, and each day without her brought more and more pain. My wolf was trying to claw his way out of me half the time, desperate to search for Neera, certain he could find her when no one else could.

So two weeks passed, until Aymeric got a call one day from the guards at the front gate while he and my brother and I were in my office, trying to discuss pack business in between waves of my pain.

He ended the call and looked at me steadily.

"Alpha," he said calmly, "Neera's back."

Chapter 5: I Was Worried

There are many things in life I had trouble believing.

For instance, I found it incomprehensible that anyone could prefer milk chocolate to dark chocolate. That just wasn't right.

I also couldn't believe that, at one time in history, mullets, leg warmers, plaid bellbottoms and beehive hairdos were actually a thing.

But mostly, I couldn't believe that my car was currently headed back to Aibek pack lands. The two weeks that Raevyn had worked with me had gone quickly.

She'd given me some potions, she'd cast some spells and then she'd wait a day or two to see how my pain was before trying something new since nothing seemed to be helping.

On the plus side, the pain didn't seem to be any worse than it was those first few days. My sleep was still interrupted by bad dreams, but they weren't as vivid, nor were they as terrifying. In my latest dreams, Night was hunting me, both as wolf and as man, but I always woke up just as he found me. So, in that sense, the sleeping remedies Raevyn was giving me were working. I wasn't waking up terrified, shaking and sweating from the horrific images plaguing my dreams. Now, I would just come awake with a gasp, calling Night's name.

Raevyn would search my eyes in the morning and frown at what she read there.

"These always worked before," she'd mutter as she considered her herbs and tried different combinations. "It must be the Alpha and Howl combination -- stronger than anything I've ever seen."

Owena, Echo and I explored her acres, full of rolling hills and trees, both as humans and as our fur girls. One memorable day, we even hunted with Blaisall's wolf, a timid, white-furred creature who seemed uneasy to be roaming, always casting about for new scents, ears up and alert for any unnatural noise. She seemed glad to shift back into Blaisall, and I felt terrible that her wolf didn't rejoice in the freedom of running and playing in the woods as our three wolves did.

"She's just old," Blaisall explained. "And I think having Raevyn inside of her makes her skittish. That's a lot of magic trapped inside of one little wolf. Honestly, I don't think Raevyn likes it, either, because when my wolf is out, her magic doesn't work, so I think Raevyn's discomfort makes my girl uneasy."

For most of our two weeks, we saw Raevyn, and only rarely did Blaisall move her aside. "I know you need her," she'd told us. "I don't want you to think I don't want to be with you, but Raevyn needs to be out so she can try to help you."

But at the end of two weeks, Raevyn had to admit defeat. "I'm only barely managing your pain as it it, Neera. Right now, I'm holding it at bay, but pushing back the pain of an Alpha rejection is like trying to hold back a tsunami with a cardboard wall. It's only temporary. It won't last. I can give you the sleeping herbal potion and show you what you need to make it, but I'm afraid that's the best I can do. I've used all of my strongest spells that should have helped, but the pain is getting around them, especially in the day time."

I tried to mask my dismay and pressed my hand to hers. "You tried your hardest. I appreciate everything you've done."

"I'm so sorry, child," she said sadly. "I thought I could help you more."

"Raevyn, honestly, I don't want you to feel bad. I've never seen anyone try harder to help a complete stranger. I can't even express how much I appreciate it."

She gave me a small smile and patted my hand. "If I didn't know better, I'd say there was some magie maléfique involved."

"What's that?" Echo asked.

"A magic that no longer exists," she said with a shudder. "And be thankful for that. It was pure evil."

"It's that much stronger than...any other magic?" I asked.

"Nothing should be stronger than the pull of a Destined One. Nothing," she explained to the three of us after dinner. "Not even my magic could prevent that kind of pull. It's its own special magic, so even if there was magic involved, Night should have been able to resist it. Only an evil magick using magie maléfique could overcome the sheer force of the Destined One, but the evil magicks were the first to be taken out by the wolves all those years ago. Not one was left alive and the magie maléfique died with them. The wolves made sure of that before they came after the good magicks."

Considering the three of us didn't even know any magic or magicks had ever existed, this was a strange and frightening world Raevyn had lived in hundreds of years ago.

"There is only one thing left to do with the pain, Neera. But you won't like it."

"Does this involve removing her brain or anything?" Owena asked. To be honest, I'd been a little afraid that Raevyn's solution was going to be something a little grisly, too, like tearing my heart out of my chest and replacing it with a rock.

Raevyn shot Owena a horrified look. "No. But maybe something almost as extreme from Neera's point of view."

"OK, tell me. I'm ready," I said as I closed my eyes, my body tense.

"You have to go back," she said quietly.

Owena jumped up, her chair skidding away from her with a screech.

Echo clapped her hands over her mouth as if she was trying to prevent herself from throwing up.

Me? My eyes popped open. "No," I said firmly. "No. I can't go back there. He'll kill me. And even if he doesn't, seeing them together will kill me. I could even survive being a zeta, I think, but seeing them together will just...will just...no. I can't do that."

"You must," Raevyn said, just as firmly. "Being near to him will help with the pain. Between proximity and my sleeping remedy, you will be able to survive."

I huffed out a short laugh. "Survive. My life has become such a joke that the best I can hope for is to survive. This rejection is the birthday gift that just keeps on giving."

"We'll figure this out," Owena vowed. "We'll go to human doctors and see if some of their strong medicines can --"

"No," Raveyn said. "That will not help Neera. And if you two loyal friends really do want to help her, you must make sure she goes back. If she does not...well, if she does not, Neera will eventually perish."

"Great! I perish if I don't go back, I perish if I do go back. Is there a third option, by any chance? Like, can't I stay here with you?"

"I'm only keeping it at bay," she told me again. "Even my magic can't do much more and it won't last forever."

For a long, long time, I looked down at the table, wondering if this is how people felt when they were sentenced to death long ago and had to walk out to face their executioner. Going back would mean my death. My wolf was sweet, but I'd discovered two weeks ago that she thought of Night as hers and she'd fight anyone who said otherwise, fight anyone who tried to take our mate or even put their hands on him.

Only the Alpha decree had kept me from attacking Lindsay Morgan, but now? No such decree existed.

Fine. Living like this wasn't living. I'd go back, a Howl returning to the Alpha who rejected her, and I'd do my best to keep my wolf suppressed and live my life as best I could...as a freaking zeta, no less...until I could take no more and my wolf broke free.

When I looked up, Raevyn, Echo and Owena were looking at me with varying expressions of pity and compassion.

No.

"We'll head back tomorrow morning," I said. "We'll be home in two days."

So, the next morning, we said goodbye to Blaisall, and then we said goodbye to Raevyn. "Thank you for everything," I said as I hugged her. "I appreciate everything you've done for me."

"Good luck to you, child," she said, her mouth set. Then she hugged me again and whispered some last-minute advice in my ear.

Goodbyes over, we piled into the car, Owena driving the first shift. She honked as we pulled away, and we began our journey back to the pack lands.

We barely said five words the rest of the day, each of us lost in thought.

The next day was a little better, but as we grew closer to the pack lands, we stopped talking again. Complete silence reigned for the last twenty miles until I was pulling up to the gates. The guard looked surprised when he saw me.

"Howl," he said, addressing me with a respectful nod as if Night hadn't rejected me.

"That's rejected Howl to you," I corrected him with the tiny little bit of spirit I had left.

I doubted it would last long. At some point on the way home, I'd realized I could be in quite a bit of trouble beyond just being rejected. As a zeta, I wasn't allowed to leave pack lands, and I'd not only left, I'd left without permission from the Alpha's Teeth.

The guard waved us through the gates, and we drove -- once again in silence -- to the apartment complex where we all lived.

After I parked, I sat back in my seat. Staring straight ahead, I swallowed. "I just want to thank you two for going with me and standing by me through all of this. You are everything best friends should be, and so much more. I will never forget --"

"Stop it. Please just stop and don't say anything else," Owena ordered, her voice thick as she pleaded with me.

"We'd do it again," Echo sniffled from the back seat. "Just know that."

I nodded, unable to speak, and then we all got out of the car.

"Holy shit!" Owena burst out, grabbing my arm and directing my attention behind us. "Alpha wolf dead ahead, coming in straight for you."

A wolf is a beautiful creature. An Alpha wolf, twice as large as most others, faster, stronger, more ferocious, was a breathtaking sight.

He was coming to kill me. I knew it. He was running full out, and I'd only been on pack lands for three minutes. This was a wolf on a mission.

To kill me.

I stood tall, unwilling to let him see my fear. He could probably smell it anyway.

Then my ride or die friends did something so foolish, so dangerous, I couldn't believe it. They shifted and stepped in front of me, their message clear.

Not today, Alpha.

As if the two of them could stop him from killing them with one swipe of his mighty paw.

Ten feet from me, Night shifted and stood in front of me, naked and just as beautiful as when he was wolf. Muscled, amazing arms crossed over his broad chest, thick thighs braced.

"Away," he gave the decree to Owena and Echo, and though they whined, they had no choice but to obey and they moved back from me.

In three long strides he was in front of me, his hands grabbing my arms, those golden eyes searching mine until I looked away. Never would I look into his eyes again, remembering all too well those delicious connections being built between us -- until he'd shattered them.

"Where have you been? Are you OK?" His voice, as was often the case after a male shifted, was deep and guttural, sometimes seeming to belong more to a wolf than to a man.

Trying to shake off his hands, I became frustrated when he wouldn't let go.

"I've been looking all over for you. I sent out teams to track you the minute I realized you'd left. Were you taken? Or did you leave on your own?"

There is something about being the focus of an Alpha's intensity. It's overwhelming, it's disorienting and it's a little bit scary. The kind of power I was facing had never in my life been directed at me, and I didn't like it.

"On my own," I stammered. "I left on my own."

"Don't do that again," he commanded me.

"Right," I said, still looking at the ground. "Because zetas can't leave pack lands. Got it."

He made a noise that sounded a lot like impatience and gripped my arms a little tighter.

"Because I was worried," he snapped. "Two weeks I didn't know where you were. None of the teams I sent out could find you, not one single trace of you. I didn't know if you were alive."

"Well, I'm sure that was a huge concern while you were busy fucking Lindsay Morgan."

Shit! I did not just throw that in my Alpha's face. I must have had a death wish, trying to accelerate the inevitable or something, because taking that tone with the Alpha would normally spell lesson time.

"Look at me," he said.

But strangely, he didn't make it a decree.

Which meant I didn't have to obey. So I didn't.

"Look at me," he repeated, more forcefully this time, but still not as a decree. Why?

"No thanks," I tossed back at him. "Last time I was forced to look at you, I did not like the live porn show, so I'm never going to look at you again."

Ummm, where the fuck was this coming from? Why was I suddenly not afraid of this man? Was it knowing I was going to die one way or the other and the when and the how no longer mattered? They were just unimportant details that all ended at the same place: with me dead.

Then he stepped back from me and howled, long and loud. Calling every-one to the Den.

Oh, shit. He was going to execute me in front of everyone at the Den.

Then he grabbed my hand -- my hand, not my arm -- in such a strong, firm grip, that I couldn't tear my hand from his hold no matter how hard I tried.

And I tried.

He pulled me after him, and I glanced over my shoulder to see Owena and Echo following, their wolves trotting after me, exchanging worried glances.

"Why are you doing this?" I asked him, suddenly realizing I didn't want to die today. "Please don't. I'll be good."

He didn't stop, but something in my tone must have broken through to him.

"What do you think is happening?" he asked me, just a hint of concern in his tone.

"You're taking me to the Den to kill me," I choked out.

"No," he said, walking faster. "I have an announcement to make and I need you there for it."

Chapter 6: Your Little Bitch

When I was a little girl, a couple of years before my parents were killed, I remember a pack event -- a summer solstice picnic that ended in a run -- and seeing our Alpha and his Howl walking hand-in-hand. He was talking to the pack members, giving them his free hand for a moment as Night and Nerón followed behind. Alpha never let go of his wife's hand. Not once. He couldn't stop touching her. All Destined Ones had a close relationship, touch and scent being especially important to us, but Alpha seemed especially linked to his Howl, never letting go of her hand once in all the time I watched.

And I watched for a long time. To this day, I couldn't say why I had followed the two of them so intently with my eyes, but I remember thinking the link between them was beautiful and pure and very, very real. It almost seemed to crackle in the air around them, and it was there in every quick glance and every longing look between them. They may have been Destined Ones, and therefore predisposed to be attracted to one another, drawn together, linked forever, but they also had come to love each other deeply.

How they raised Night in that kind of loving, openly adoring environment only to have him turn out to be a man who could humiliate and debase his own Howl was a mystery to me -- and most likely to our pack members. Even if Destined Ones didn't love each other, at the very least there was great affection, mutual respect and deep caring.

Now for the second time in two weeks, I was being dragged to the Den, but this time Night was leading me by the hand instead of my upper arm. And once again, this time I had no idea what was about to go down.

Maybe my execution? Could he actually do that to me, his Howl, his very own Destined One sent by the Forces? The thought seemed impossible -- yet so had his rejection of me, and he had done that without blinking. My thoughts kept circling wildly, yet my execution seemed to be his most likely course of action.

If he was going to kill me, though, he might very well have a revolt on his hands. If the bonds between Destined Ones were sacred, the bond between the Alpha and Howl were revered. I already knew from the silence following my rejection that the wolves weren't happy with him. Wolves are not quiet creatures in their joy and happiness; that there was such complete silence when he sent me away from him was telling. Nobody except Lindsay Morgan had been pleased with Night that day.

Now, if he was going to rip my throat out, I wanted Owena and Echo far away from here. They'd shifted right before they walked into the Den, just on my heels, and they were whispering together, as near to me as they could get. Probably trying to figure out how they could possibly save me if Night was about to end my life.

Unfortunately, if they attempted to stop him or in any way interfere with his decision to execute me, their lives would be forfeit. They would end up with their throats being torn out, too. No one could stand in the way of an execution unless they wanted to end up dead.

As Night continued to drag me toward the fireplace where the first scene of my humiliation had taken place, my eyes searched the room for Lindsay Morgan's sure-to-be-smirking face. Maybe she was hidden away, ready to make her grand entrance at just the perfect moment.

I declare my loyalty to Lindsay Morgan, and it is to her that I declare my allegiance and my devotion.

I know it was unreasonable to hate her, but I did. She knew she was not his Destined One, but she held Night's heart, so much so that he resisted the strong pull of his Howl.

So I state here and now, with all of our pack as witnesses, that I reject Neera Karis. I reject her as my Destined One. I reject her as my Howl.

He had told every member of our pack that somehow, he did not feel anything for me. That there was nothing between us that he could sense, that I may have been any other wolf to him. Nothing special.

I find no joy in this one. There is nothing within me that feels the pull of the bond, that she is truly my Destined One.

In effect, Night was telling everyone in our pack that the Forces that had joined us together long ago had made a mistake. He'd thrown me over for Lindsay Morgan, a woman most definitely not marked as his own. Where was she? She wouldn't want to miss my execution. Maybe she was trying to find just the right outfit for watching the Alpha's Howl get killed. Holy shit -- maybe he was going to let her tear my throat out. What a statement that would make to the pack. Lindsay Morgan may not have been his Destined One, but by allowing that action, she would be made his queen.

"So, where's your little bitch?" I snapped at him when my thoughts became too much to hold inside. Maybe I could provoke him into just ending this before Lindsay Morgan made her grand entrance. I'd prefer Night to kill me -- then my blood would be on lips if he ever came to regret his actions.

"She is not your concern," he answered me gruffly, then said no more.

Well, if she wasn't my concern, maybe that meant she wasn't going to be the one to kill me.

Look at me, still trying to find the rainbow among the clouds.

Night turned me to face the room, and I noticed all of the wolves gathering, some running into the room as wolves and shifting immediately, panting, curious, nervous. I could sense all of the emotions rolling off of my pack mates in waves, and I suddenly knew they were behind me. They didn't want to witness another clusterfuck -- literally -- like they did two weeks ago.

Soon the room was almost at capacity, and I scanned it again, over and over, but still couldn't see Lindsay Morgan, not even at the farthest edges of the crowd.

As the last wolves came running like crazy to get here, I wondered what they were thinking. Were they wondering if they were about to witness history in the making yet again? Were they thinking that maybe they were about to watch an Alpha executing his Howl? Or did something that outrageous not even occur to them?

Once again, I tried tugging my hand away from his, but he shot me a glance. "Stop," he said in a no-nonsense tone I'd heard him use with some older delta boys on occasion when their roughhousing with the younger delta boys was getting too rough.

However, since it still wasn't issued as a decree, I didn't stop struggling.

Night leaned down and whispered in my ear. "Stop."

"Fuck you," I said just as softly, and he reared back, probably never having been spoken to like that before by a pack member, even before he became

Alpha. Night and his wolf were scary as hell; add the Alpha ferocity and power and this man was someone you did not want to mess with.

"Fine. You're just humiliating yourself in front of the pack with your actions."

Did he just --

Had I heard --

Was he kidding --

Oh, hell no!

"You asshole," I hissed at him. "I have never humiliated myself in front of the pack. You did that to me all on your own with your precious girlfriend."

Hmmm. If the look on his face was anything to go by, maybe I was on the fast track to provoking him into tearing out my throat and making my execution quick and (relatively) painless.

Instead of responding to me, or even turning his head toward me, he just started in on addressing all of the assembled wolves.

"Two weeks ago, you all witnessed my rejection of Neera Karis as my Howl."

He let his words settle over the crowd for a minute. Ah, such fond memories for all of us as a pack. I tugged at my hand again, not wanting to be touching him as he walked us all through the day I'd much rather forget. How the hell could I ever think of that day again without remembering that it was also the same day that my Destined One not only rejected me, but did so in the most horrifying, humiliating, brutal way?

From the disgusted and angry looks on the faces of my pack mates, it seemed they would also rather not relive the day. Since I'd been forced to watch the brutal scene, forced to keep my eyes on Night and what he was doing to Lindsay Morgan, I hadn't been able to look at my pack mates' reactions.

Owena and Echo had filled me in on the looks of loathing and hate focused on Night and Lindsay, of everyone's extreme distaste for and discomfort with the scene. And like I'd said before, public nudity and public sex didn't bother us in the least. It was just the way we wolves rolled. But this instance of public sex had been wrong, it went against nature, against the Forces. And it was used to teach me a horrible lesson.

"And after I rejected her, I made her zeta."

At those words, something in me lifted. Hope began flickering in my chest that maybe today wasn't going to be the day that my Alpha, my Destined One, ripped out my throat. Maybe, just maybe, there was an outside chance that this announcement was to reinstate me as a gamma. That was why he needed me here! That kind of announcement was much better than notice of my execution.

"She is no longer zeta."

Oh, please don't let him say that now I'm even lower than the zetas. That just wasn't possible.

"I say this now in front of you as my witnesses, Neera Karis is my Howl. I accept her as my Destined One, as the Howl sent to me by the Forces in their wisdom."

What?

Two weeks ago, he railed Lindsay Morgan in front of me, in front of all of us, to reject me as his Destined One...and now he was doing a one-eighty and announcing to everyone that I'm his Howl after all? Oops, he made a mistake by rejecting me, by fucking Lindsay Morgan like his life depended on it, like it was his job, and then demoting me to zeta for no reason other than the sheer audacity of me having been revealed as his Howl? Two weeks ago he rejected me, and in so doing, consigned me to a life of pain -- however long it lasted -- since he hadn't issued a decree ordering me not to attack Lindsay Morgan.

Did I just hear him right?

I looked over at Owena and Echo, and they were slack jawed, exactly as I felt, so I must have heard Night correctly.

Pardon me if I was feeling a little whiplashed.

And pissed.

Two weeks ago, this man, my Alpha, my Destined One, put me through hell, and now he was doing a motherfucking take-backsie?

No.

Even the most mild of us have our breaking points, and my limit had just been reached.

"No. No!" I shouted at Night, and everyone froze.

You did not talk to the Alpha like that, not unless you wanted a lesson in respect.

"Right here in this room, two weeks ago, you denied the pull of the Destined Ones when nothing, and I mean nothing, should have been able to keep you from me. Not even the love you have for Lindsay Morgan should have kept you from me. Nothing could have kept you from me, from your Destined One, your Howl!"

Night took a step toward me, to do what, I had no idea, so I popped my hand up to stop him. It was laughable, really, acting as if I had the power to keep him from me -- but he stopped.

Then I looked around the room at all the wolves who were witness to my humiliation on my birthday, and then I looked back at him but not at his stupid face.

"So, Alpha, having already made your choice in front of all these witnesses two weeks ago, now it's my turn to make my choice. I formally reject you as my Destined One. I reject you on the basis of a weak bond that could not stand up to another woman, a bond you destroyed through your despicable actions and did not fight for. I reject the mate brand. I reject being your Howl. And most of all, Night Slaine, I forever reject you."

Chapter 7: She Was Eyeing My Throat

What the ever living fuck had just happened? My Howl had just rejected me? After I brought her back to the Den to right the wrong that had been done to her two weeks ago? How the hell had that happened?

The silence in the room was absolute, half the eyes on me, wondering what I was going to do; the other half on the back of my Howl as she walked toward the doors to leave the Den.

At the very least, I was her Alpha, and that should have prevented her defiance, but the fact that she was my Destined One, my fucking Howl, should have kept her glued to my side. Possibly looking up at me adoringly, but I could wait for that as long as she stayed by my side for the time being.

Instead, I watched her walking away from me, that soft, rounded ass twitching enticingly as she stalked out the doors. Once she was gone, the other half of the pack's eyes turned to me, so now every single member was silently questioning me: what's your next move, Alpha?

Not sure why they were treating this like some kind of damn soap opera, but wolves were a fucking nosy bunch who lived for drama and gossip.

My wolf was ready and raring to go because Neera had broken rule number one when dealing with a predator: never turn your back on one. I saw the door close behind her, still stunned that she'd rejected me in front of the pack. In three strides I was running after her -- shifting the second I was outside the doors -- and my wolf was after her immediately, following her delicious scent that made him want to give her his belly.

Unbelievable. I was Alpha -- I didn't roll on my back for anyone, yet here my wolf was ready to give her his belly. Weak bastard. But fuck! She smelled so good.

She'd obviously shifted the second she'd walked outside the Den and taken off, and although she was out of sight, I could track her easily. Neera's wolf was a pretty little fur-girl, but she was tiny compared to my beast, and my legs ate up the distance between us, following her scent -- god, that fucking scent was doing things to me -- and after a couple of minutes, I had her in my sight.

Her head turned to gauge the distance and she took off, darting for some bushes that she could get through much more easily than I could, but could still scratch her up and tear at her fur and skin.

Unacceptable.

With a burst of power, I hit her from behind, shifting in a split second to wrap my arms around her little wolf, keeping her safe while I rolled us to a stop.

We ended up with me on my back -- damned if my belly wasn't exposed, after all -- and her wolf snapped her jaws right in my face, making me laugh.

"No, Neera," I reprimanded her gently, my fingers rubbing her neck.

She did it again, though, three more times in fact, and I was roaring with laughter, feeling free for the first time in years. How had I rejected her? There was no way. Just no way I could have done that. Everything about her called to me, called to my wolf, drew us to her.

Then she lunged for my throat, holding it firmly in her jaws, taking me completely by surprise with that bold and foolish action.

I'm in love, my wolf sighed to me. Useless bastard.

"You need to let go," I told her gently but firmly. "I can't allow your fur-girl to get away with much more, Neera."

Instead of listening to me, she bit down a little harder, this time her teeth sinking into my neck enough to draw a little blood.

Could she be any more perfect?

My wolf needed to shut the fuck up. It was one thing being indulgent of your Destined One; it was another thing entirely to let her be in a position that allowed her to rip your throat out -- that could definitely fuck with your relationship and any chance of future happiness if one of you was, say, dead.

I could shift, and the size of my neck would automatically make her loosen her grip on me, but I wanted to let this play out, knowing I could stop her in a second if I needed to. But most of all, I wanted to see how far she'd go, how long we'd be at this standoff, how this would end. Would she end it, or would I? I wanted her to stop it; I wanted her to submit to me.

But as usual, lately, the Forces were going to fuck with me.

We'd stayed like that for ten fucking minutes, me stroking her fur, trying to see if I could relax her enough to get her to let go.

"You're so beautiful, Neera. Your fur-girl is gorgeous. You're both pretty girls," I crooned to her.

Life lesson -- I should have left it at that. But did I? No. Of course not. She may be my Howl, my Destined One, but there was still a lot I needed to learn about my Neera.

"You need to shift, so I can fuck you and we can Take the Blood," I said softly. Enticingly, I thought.

She thought differently. With a growl, she tried to deepen the bite, and I shifted so fast her jaws flew off my throat. She shifted back to Neera, and I did the same, pinning her to the ground on her stomach, my hard cock pressing against her ass.

There is no position a shifter loves more, and her defiance, her holding my throat in her jaws? Foreplay.

"Neera," I started to say, my voice pitched to soothe her.

"No," she told me, interrupting whatever I had been about to say. She was so vulnerable now, completely at my mercy, and still she had the strength, the guts, to tell me no. "Get off me, Night. Get off me."

She's fucking awesome, my wolf howled in approval.

"I will," I promised, "but just know if you try to run, I will catch you, and I will make sure you won't run from me again. When I get off of you, I want you to sit up and face me so we can talk."

Never had I wanted to use an Alpha Decree on someone so badly, but I refused to do that to her. My father had raised me to believe that the power I held should never be misused or overused, and above all should never be used on my Destined One.

"If you can only rule and command obedience with Decrees, you aren't worth the title of Alpha," he'd told me many times. He'd been a great Alpha, and his legacy was one I hoped to live up to and to one day pass on to my son who would be born to rule the pack.

I'd given Neera fair warning of what I wanted to happen and what the consequences would be if she chose not to listen, so what happened next was all up to her. I'd always known her to be a typical gamma wolf -- mild, obedient, never making waves, ready to listen to me just because I was her Alpha. I wasn't exactly sure what had happened to that Neera -- had my rejection of her created an entirely new Neera? -- but my wolf loved the new version of her that we'd never seen before.

She sure as shit was exhibiting Howl tendencies now. Growing up, the only one in the pack not afraid of my father was my mother. In fact, she ruled him. Never in public, but at home, she gave him her opinion and told him in no uncertain terms when he'd been an idiot. Often. And my father listened to her and worked to regain her favor, her smile. He'd often shift to wolf and bare his belly to her in apology and she'd stand over him, arms crossed, looking down at this ridiculously huge beast of a wolf whose tongue was hanging out, his wolf-eyes pleading as he whined forgive me. Then she would roll her eyes, huff out her exasperation and bend down to rub his belly. Immediately, he'd shift back, grab her hand and disappear into their bedroom to read books. Yes. Read books and nothing more. That's what I always told myself because...fucking gross. Just not going there. Wolves saw sex all the time, it happened in public and no one thought anything of it...unless it was your parents.

I suspected, but wasn't quite ready to admit, that Neera would be my only weakness just like my mother was my father's. I'd command the pack, and she would command me.

As I slowly removed my weight from Neera, I sat back on the grass and watched to see what she would do. For a moment or two, she remained on her stomach, then she sat up and turned to face me, her face varying shades of pissed off.

"Good girl," I praised her.

Her eyes narrowed on me.

"Now, let's start with what happened in the Den today. Why did you reject me when I decided to take you as my Howl?"

I went over the words in my head and found not one thing wrong with what I'd said.

I say this now in front of you as my witnesses, Neera Karis is my Howl. I accept her as my Destined One, as the Howl sent to me by the Forces in their wisdom.

"Are you fucking serious?" she demanded. "You wonder how I could reject you? You rejected me first! You stood there right in front of every single member of our pack and rejected me as your Destined One, as your Howl, even though the evidence was staring you right in the face with our matching mate brands. And then, oh, and then! You proceeded to fuck Lindsay Morgan right in front of me. Since my humiliation wasn't quite complete, as if what you'd already done just wasn't enough, you made me a zeta! The lowest of the low in the pack! For no reason other than to be mean and humiliate me all the way into the dust."

"Well, I don't remember that. Any of it, other than what people told me. So let's move past that bullshit and focus on today. Once I was ready to announce you as my Howl --"

"Bullshit?"

Her voice was suddenly very growly and she was eyeing my throat again.

"Focus on the now, Neera, not on what happened. That's the past. We need to work this out in the now. It's hurting the pack if the Alpha and his Howl are at odds."

"And why are we at odds? Because of what you did to me! That's why we're at odds! You never even addressed it with me, you just marched your happy ass to the Den, dragging me along once again -- but at least your girlfriend wasn't there this time! -- and without even telling me your plans, without an apology or an explanation as to what happened on my birthday, which, for the record, was the shittiest birthday ever, and you thought I was going to fall all over myself when you suddenly did a complete turnaround and accepted me as your Howl? Are you fucking insane?"

This having to explain myself was going to take some getting used to, but since Neera was my Howl, I could adapt. Going from not having to justify yourself to anyone to having to explain yourself to your Howl was going to be an adjustment. She just needed to be patient with me and show me some understanding.

I breathed out a huge lungful of air and stared at Neera. "I'm sorry about what happened two weeks ago. I have no idea what happened to make me reject you and do all that other shit. I'm ready to accept you as my Howl."

She stared at me, anger still brewing in those eyes, clearly expecting...more?

"Oh! And I'm sorry your birthday was shitty. I'll buy you something nice to make up for it."

Neera surged to her feet, and I did, too, afraid she was going to bolt.

"That's it? That's my apology, my explanation for the most humiliating, excruciatingly painful day of my life? Not forgetting the extremely generous offer of buying me something nice to make up for the sheer hell you put me through?"

I looked at her for a minute, clearly lost. I was missing something here. I'd given her more explanation than I'd ever given in my life as Alpha, and frankly, since I didn't remember my actions in the Den that day, I wasn't sure what more she wanted.

"I'm not sure what more you want, but if you tell me, I'll give it to you."

"Oh my -- for fuck's sake, Night! I want you to leave me alone for tonight! Right now, I'm so pissed off, I want to tear your throat out and roast it over a fire while your bloody carcass gets torn apart by buzzards. In lieu of that, I just want to go back to my apartment and settle down so that tomorrow we can talk about this like rational people and I don't just sit there, watching your mouth move, while I think of all the ways I'd like to kill you slowly and painfully!"

Takeaway: she wanted to talk tomorrow. That was a start.

Yes! Progress!

Chapter 8: Your Cozy Nest

Was he freaking kidding me? He was going to buy me a nice present? That would make everything better and I'd forget about what he did to me? Our pack might need a new Alpha if he was delusional enough to think I could be bribed into forgiveness by a nice present.

You know what a nice present would be, Alpha? Your head mounted to a piece of wood over my fireplace. That would be a nice present, you idiot, I thought as I shoved some clothes into a small duffle bag. I had to get out of here, and this time, Owena and Echo couldn't go with me. Three would be easier to track than one, and this time I suspected -- even with the potions Raevyn had taught me to make -- the pain would quickly become unbearable the farther away I got from Night, until the only option left was crawling under some thick bushes and letting the agony overwhelm me until it stopped my heart. I didn't want my friends to see that, to feel the helplessness of watching me writhe and twist in pain, unable to help. They would stay with me every excruciating moment, and I loved them too much to let them watch me die like that.

Stupid Alpha, I thought as I recalled him announcing his acceptance of me as his Howl to our assembled pack mates. I'd felt a weird combination of pissed off and warm and fuzzy when he'd said that. Obviously, my anger had won that round. He'd forced me to watch him fuck Lindsay Morgan in front of everyone only two weeks before -- and now I was supposed to just roll over and give him my belly because he'd decided he would graciously accept me as his Howl.

Well, I don't remember that. Any of it, other than what people told me. So let's move past that bullshit and focus on today.

Move past that! Just move on as if he hadn't ripped my heart out of my chest.

Focus on the now, Neera, not on what happened. That's the past. We need to work this out in the now. It's hurting the pack if the Alpha and his Howl are at odds.

Such a typical Alpha attitude and approach to life. Because I have said so, jump to obey me, no explanations needed or given!

I hoped he wasn't thinking clearly right now -- hoped he didn't think I would sing a song I'd already sung and run away again.

Woof! This day was taking its toll on me and it wasn't even fucking noon. In the space of three hours, I'd returned to pack lands, certain I was going to be killed; I'd been confronted by my delusional Alpha and announced as his Howl in front of the pack; I'd rejected said delusional Alpha; I'd been chased down by him so he could tell me to get over the events from two weeks ago, and then I'd begged for some time so I could think tonight and he and I could talk tomorrow.

Lie! I'd hoped to be long gone by the time tomorrow rolled around.

I ignored the fact that for three hours, just from being in his proximity, my pain had dissipated completely. When we'd been naked, with me on my belly and him on top of me, I'd wanted him to take me, to make me his, to take my blood so I could take his. I'd thought how easy it would have been for him to plunge inside of me and fuck me harder than he'd ever fucked anyone in his life, harder than I'd ever been fucked in my life, and to fill me with a gift only he could give to me.

But he'd resisted the call of my body and his -- there was no way he could have missed how wet I was for that hard, delicious cock he'd had pressed against me. For a split second, we were Alpha and Howl, the most potent combination there was in our world, and it would have been so, so easy to just forget what had happened and give in to our primitive, animalistic natures.

Somehow, I'd resisted, told him no and amazingly, he'd listened. When a male was faced with his Destined One in that position, it took some amazing control not to let his instincts push him into getting me ready for him, making me want to submit. He was Alpha and I was his Howl; I was genetically predisposed to want to submit to him, to take his cock, to give him those pups only I could give to him and only he could give to me.

He'd backed off even though we both knew it would have taken very little coaxing on his part to get me to welcome him into my body.

But I'd shaken off the fuck haze and bought myself some time to get away from him.

Since my other bag was already in the car, I hadn't needed to pack much in this one. Just some things I hadn't grabbed the first time I ran away. I looked around my apartment, then walked out for the last time. I wouldn't be coming back.

I threw the bag in my trunk, and drove toward the front gate.

Unlike last time, this time my car was stopped and I had to think fast.

"I'm on a mission!" I sang out to the guard. "Alpha accepted me as his Howl, and our ceremony's going to be tonight! Tonight! Can you believe it?" I gushed to him.

He smiled. "I'm glad to hear that, Howl. That was a bad business two weeks ago."

You know what' else is going to be a bad business? You not letting me out of here!

"Well, this is all very hush hush, but I'm on my way to get my dress for the ceremony tonight. Night's so impatient he wouldn't wait one more night! So I really need to get going so I can find a dress and get back here in time for the ceremony. Your Alpha's not going to be happy if I can't find a dress and I make him wait until I can find one!"

The guard looked a little pale at that, and with a smile, waved me through the gate. I waited until I was out of sight before flooring it, taking some sharp turns until I was heading in the opposite direction the guard had seen me go. I drove and drove, and with each mile, a little bit of the pain came creeping back. By the time I stopped at some skeevy hotel that accepted cash, the pain was crashing over me in waves, and I was exhausted.

I ordered a small pizza, had it delivered to my door and ate it despite the pain. I made the potion to help me sleep, and I got a few hours before I knew trying to sleep any longer was useless. My fingers itched to call Echo and Owena, but I'd left my phone behind just in case they could somehow track it. So I left and hit the road again, driving aimlessly, heading north today instead of west. Focusing on my driving helped, but the pain was ever-present.

For three weeks, I drove all over the country in an aimless pattern, and each day, the pain came at me a little harder, and my dreams at night grew more and more vivid. In them, Night was searching for me as both man and wolf. His wolf was howling for me, and my wolf howled in return. Sad. Mournful. Angry at their human halves for keeping them apart. When it was Night searching for me, his eyes were sad and tortured.

"I am nothing but pain without you," he called to me every time I managed to sleep for a few hours. "Tell me where you are, Neera. Neera! I'll come for you!"

My dreams only served to increase the pain. Startled awake, I'd get up, leave the hotel and drive to a wooded area where I could let my fur-girl run.

That helped the pain more than anything, but she often lifted her face to the sky to howl out her agony and despair to Night's wolf, who was, depending on the day, anywhere between two hundred and a thousand miles away. Then we would run and run and run until we were so exhausted, we'd hide under some bushes and sleep a little until we woke before sunrise. We'd run back to the car, shift, dress and take off in the car for another fun-filled day of driving around in whatever direction called to me that day.

I half expected to see Raevyn waiting for me on some rocks as my fur-girl ran in the woods, but she never appeared. Honestly, I wasn't terribly surprised; she had done all she could for me before. There was nothing Raevyn could do now.

Some days, I felt as if I could live with the pain; then others, it would be so debilitating I could barely think or drive. The good days, I discovered, were precursors to the pain taking a turn for the worse, so I began to dread the good days. It was a miserable existence and I often thought about letting my fur-girl have dominance forever. The pain wasn't as bad with her pushed forward, but I guessed that would just be a matter of time, too, before she was overtaken by the pain.

I'd ordered my usual pizza on what I'd determined to be my last night in the hotel. My money was running out and since I didn't sleep much anyway, why not just sleep in the woods? Owena and Echo would be horrified -- it's not safe, Neera! -- but nothing scared me any longer. If something were to happen, well...the thought was no longer frightening, or at least no more frightening than the thought of facing the worsening pain.

The burning hot shower I'd taken just after putting in my pizza order helped. I'd scrubbed my hair clean and then my body, enjoying the feel of the pain receding a bit in the face of the shower's heat.

I got out of the shower, listening for the knock at the door that would signal the arrival of my dinner. With the extra towel, I dried my hair, then threw on some gray sweats and a soft purple hoodie. While I waited, I clicked through the TV channels, glad my pain had almost disappeared from the hot shower, allowing me to concentrate on the show for once.

Knock knock knock!

I jumped up and looked out the peephole. There was my pizza delivery man with all that meat-lover's goodness. Normally, I wasn't that hungry from the pain, but tonight, without the pain to suppress my appetite, I was starving.

I opened the door and accepted my pizza, handed him the money with a thank you and stepped back inside.

Just as a huge hand hit my door and pushed it wide open.

"Hello, Neera," Night flashed me his teeth and it was quite obviously not a smile.

After he walked into the room, he pushed the door shut behind him, then turned to face me, arms crossed over his chest.

"No welcome for me, sweet girl?"

Again with that feral grin.

No wonder my pain had disappeared; Night had been close.

Shit.

He was blocking the door. I could try to crash through the window, but he was bigger, stronger, faster and he would never let me get that close since I could hurt myself. Male wolves were obsessively protective of their Destined Ones.

"What do you want?" I demanded.

OK, that feral grin had to go because I did not like it. At all.

"Just to spend some time with my Destined One," he said innocently in a voice that was anything but. "I hear you've been dress shopping, but I can't believe you couldn't find one single dress that you liked in the last three weeks for our Blood ceremony. I never knew you were that particular, my little fur-girl."

Instead of answering, I crossed my arms over my chest and waited him out.

"You might want to eat your pizza because once we're in the car, my precious lambchop, I'm not stopping until we're back on pack lands."

We were three hundred miles from the pack lands!

Deliberately, ignoring my growling stomach, I dumped the pizza into the wastebasket. No male wolf would deny his Destined One food.

Shaking his head, Night disapproved of my impulsiveness.

"While I want to care for you and meet your needs, darling crumpet of my heart, my overriding concern is getting you back to pack lands, where I can claim you as my Howl and keep you safe."

"Good luck with that," I scoffed. "I'm not going anywhere with you."

That fucking feral grin!

"We're going back tonight, my sweet pumpkin."

"I'm not going back. I'll fight you every step of the way and if I have to, I'll jump from the car."

"Ah, sounds like foreplay to me," he quipped. "But we'll have to wait until we're back on pack lands to indulge your feisty nature that I need to subdue and conquer, my little sweet potato."

"Stop with the stupid pet names!" I practically shrieked at him. "I'm not going back with you, I'm not going to be fucking conquered, and I'm not going to become your Howl. And I'm not kidding -- I will fight you while you're driving, I will break the window and jump out if I have to, but I will not go back and I will not submit!"

I'm a wolf. I'm fast and quick.

But an Alpha?

Much faster. Much quicker.

So I was thrown over his shoulder before I could even blink and he walked us out of the hotel room and the ten steps to his car that was parked right outside the room.

Backed into the space.

He popped the trunk.

Oh, no no no no.

He wouldn't dare --

I started shrieking in earnest, but this was the type of sleazy motel where that was the norm rather than the exception, and not one single person even opened a door to see what was going on.

"Quiet," he said and delivered a sharp slap to my ass that was hard enough to make me suck in my breath and stop my screaming.

"You have waters in there, a light, and a disabled release cord so you can't open the trunk. I've also put some cushions in there so you'll be quite comfortable in your cozy nest, my little cream puff."

And with that, he dumped me into my cozy nest and shut me in the trunk.

Motherfucker was going to die.

Chapter 9: Every Last Detail

"What have we discovered?" I asked Aymeric, forcing myself not to pace, even though my wolf was prowling restlessly. We need to find her. Why are we still here?

"Nothing substantial. When I went through the ancient archives, I found two references to magicks. One was part of an alpha scroll stating that they feared the magicks, especially the magie maléfique, were going to wipe out the wolves, and then the other one said only The magicks are no more."

"I don't believe that," I said, as sure of that as I was of anything else in my life. "Some must have survived. We need to find out more. Are you sure you looked in every text?"

"Three times, Alpha. I went over every last inch of the archives for secret hiding places, in both the books and the shelves and the walls. Every piece of furniture was also checked. In many books from about 400 years ago, many of the texts are missing chunks of pages, as if they were ripped out, purged. All references to magicks and magic were destroyed except for the two that I mentioned that were overlooked."

Slamming my hand on the table, I glared at Aymeric. "I don't believe that! There must be something! What about this Raevyn? There are rumors of a woman who has magic, who can help those suffering from the rejected mate pain."

"We have asked, Alpha," Aymeric said calmly. "No one knows anything beyond rumors, except possibly Owena and Echo. When we questioned them about the Raevyn, they played dumb."

That had me snarling, and Aymeric eyed me carefully, ready to bow his head if he thought I was about to lose my shit. "I think you should talk with them."

"Decree them, you mean."

"Yes, Alpha. If even a few magicks survived and were intent on destroying the wolves back then, we should assume no less now. We need every bit of information we can get."

"Bring them to me."

When the two women were in front of me half an hour later, trembling slightly but trying to be brave, I simply looked at them and then said, "You will share with me everything you know of the Raevyn. Leave nothing out. Tell me every last detail."

For an hour, Aymeric and I listened in stunned silence, asking questions when they had finished.

"And where did you find her?" I demanded.

They explained where, and then Echo said, "But, Alpha, she found us. Unless she wants you to find her, you will not."

"Do you think Neera left to seek her out, to go back to the Raevyn's home?"

This time, Owena answered. "No. Raevyn did something to cloak her location. So only minutes after we left, we had no idea where we were. Her home was lost to us. There was only forward, to pack lands."

"Is there anything left to tell me, anything I should know? Did Neera tell you she was taking off this time?"

"No, Alpha," Echo said, fear and sincerity in every word. Being under an Alpha decree was not the most comfortable feeling for a wolf. "We were as surprised as you that she was gone."

Owena continued, "She didn't leave a note, and since she left her phone behind, we have no way to contact her."

I dismissed them with an admonishment not to share what they had told me with anyone.

When they were gone, I looked at Aymeric.

"This Raevyn shares a body. She uses potions to allow the sharing of the body and to ease the pain of rejection."

"Yes, Alpha."

"So, it's not a stretch to think that somehow, Lindsay Morgan used potions to enchant me for the last three years."

Aymeric shook his head, and I knew that we were both thinking dark thoughts.

"Or worse," he said.

"It could have been a powerful magic that allowed Lindsay Morgan to control my body that day, my thoughts, my words."

"A magic so powerful that it caused both of you to pass out once Neera left the Den. We know nothing of magic, but the power required to do that must have depleted you both."

"She used my body to fuck herself," I shuddered, disgusted but glad to know I had not rejected my Destined One, I had not fucked another woman in front of my Howl, I had not decreed her to watch. I had not made her zeta. I was blameless in the whole nasty business, if what I strongly suspected was true, but convincing my Howl of that might be tricky. What she had seen was unprecedented, something no Alpha had done to his Howl, and I imagined it might take her a while to get over it.

Now can we go?

My wolf had been at me for the week that Neera had been gone to go find her, hunt her down. I'd wanted to, but just leaving my pack to roam the country searching for Neera was not possible.

The pain was intensifying, and my dreams were becoming more and more vivid, making me frantic, a sense of urgency nipping at my heels to find her, make her ours. It was her wolf I saw in my dreams most often, howling her despair, her need for us. Sometimes Neera was in my dreams, curled into a little ball, holding her stomach, crying softly with pain.

Echo and Owena had told me that Raevyn had blocked their presence in her home so none of the trackers I had sent to find Neera could locate her. But unless Raevyn was helping Neera again, this time I had a chance of finding her. I'd sent out my eight best trackers but they'd found nothing yet in the week since she'd disappeared. Again.

We could find her. I know we could.

My wolf wanted desperately to find Neera. As Alpha, I was needed here for the well-being of my pack, but I wanted to go find my Howl just as badly as he did. Unfortunately, I couldn't be gone for weeks on end; the Alpha was critical to pack members calm, to keep the wolves steady, even if it was just a word from me or a touch of my hand every day. I had to wait to move until one of my trackers closed in on her. The pack could function without me for a couple of days.

My dreams continued for two weeks, and my wolf met Neera's fur-girl every night, and she began to show my wolf clues in her limited way. The minute I woke up, I'd call a tracker in the area that I thought she was and they'd head there during the night while she slept.

It took two more weeks, but my trackers finally located her and paid a man to put a tracker on her car.

The next day, when she stopped, she was only three hundred miles from pack lands. One of my wolves who was a pilot flew me to the closest municipal airport to Neera. I rented a car, stopped at a nearby Target to gather a few items I suspected I'd need and backed into the empty parking space right next to Neera's car. Working quickly, I readied the trunk for Neera, just in case she proved to be troublesome about returning to pack lands with me.

The ache in my chest had eased immediately since my Destined One was near. Just as I finished with the trunk, a pizza delivery man pulled up and headed for Neera's door. I casually followed him -- and the meat-lover's pizza -- to her door.

Her scent was all over the door, and I breathed deeply, relishing my Destined One's scent.

I heard Neera open her door, and as soon as the delivery man left, I stepped in front of her door and slapped my hand against it. Following her into the room, I kicked the door shut behind me.

Sniff her hair. Let's sniff her hair. She smells so good. So good. So good!

Stop, I ordered my wolf. Now was not the time.

Can we lick her face, then? I want to lick her face.

Ignoring him and his joy at being reunited with Neera, I allowed myself to relax in relief that we'd found her, but at the same time, all my bottled-up anger for the last three weeks surged to the fore. Although I forced myself not to yell at her, I did allow my displeasure to be known through the old standby of sarcasm and biting little nicknames to force a reaction from her. My Howl had left the safety of pack lands and was therefore unguarded. She could have found herself hunted by other packs or worse. My girl's wolf was on the smaller side -- lovely, but definitely not big enough to overcome most wolves. A Howl without her mate was vulnerable, and for three weeks she'd been alone. Unprotected. Vulnerable.

For a moment, I remembered my mother's wolf, returned to the pack in pieces -- No.

Since she proved unwilling, I threw Neera over my shoulder and carried her out to the car. I popped the trunk, and once she stopped her screaming, explained all the luxuries I'd put into the trunk for her comfort.

I put her into the trunk and slammed it shut. Immediately she started screaming and pounding on the trunk lid. I listened to her swearing at me for a minute.

"My parents were definitely married, Neera!" I called to her, trying not to laugh when that made her shriek even louder.

She's not happy.

To say the least. But she'd soon come to realize that this was for her own safety. She might even thank me for it if she calmed down enough to think things through.

We drove for about one hundred miles, my Howl not letting up for even a minute with the kicking and yelling. I was kind of proud of her for being so ornery, but at the same time I wished she'd settle onto the cushions and just go to sleep. The constant noise wasn't making for a fun drive.

For the hour and a half that I drove, my wolf growled at me the whole time while I listened to Neera yell and lash out with her fists and legs.

And then suddenly...utter silence.

My wolf went on alert and then we heard the faint sound of her sniffling. "Please, Night, help me. I hurt myself," she cried out to me, her voice growing more frantic with each word. "Please -- I must have cut myself and I'm bleeding bad. Ple --"

Then nothing. Not even sniffling. No sound of movement.

My wolf went nuts, and it was all I could do to hold him back. He was trying to force a shift, something he'd never done before, and given that wolves didn't have opposable thumbs, that would make driving pretty fucking difficult.

"Hold on," I snapped, fighting him back. "I'm going to get off the highway and find a safe place to pull over, you asshole!"

Two minutes later, I was off the highway, off the beaten path, and parked behind an abandoned gas station. I ran to the back of the car, still listening in vain for any sound and threw open the trunk.

Fur and fangs fucking flew out of the trunk, aiming straight for my throat, and at the last second, I caught her in my arms and held her away from me.

She's fucking perfect! my wolf howled, happy that our Destined One had just gone for our throat.

Neera's fur-girl struggled mightily, jaws snapping, desperately trying to free herself from my grip.

"Shift, Neera."

Growling, she tried to bite my hand that was stroking her neck, fighting against my hold.

"Shift so we can talk," I tried again. I refused to use an Alpha decree on her.

"Shift or I'll shift and we'll take the blood as wolves," I threatened her.

YES! YES! YES! DOOOO IT! DOOOO IT!

He really needed to calm down.

I squeezed Neera a little to show her I was serious.

I suddenly had a naked woman in my arms, a soft, curvy woman who had riled up me and my wolf. She wriggled out of my arms and turned to face me, hands on her hips.

"Are you insane?" she demanded. "In what world did you think it would be OK to lock me in a motherfucking TRUNK? You stupid asshole! I'm going to kill you when you least expect it! I can't believe you thought that would be a good move! How stupid are you that you thought kidnapping me from my hotel room would be a good idea?"

I looked at her, breathing fire and enraged, totally adorable. "You'll get over it."

Apparently, that was the wrong thing to say, even if it was the truth.

"That's your answer to everything, you idiot! Get over being rejected! Get over you forcing me to watch you fuck your long-term girlfriend! Get over being rejected in front of the pack! Get over being made a zeta! Get over it, get over it, get over it! That's all you can say, but you sure as hell haven't acknowledged the pain you put me through!"

And that, in turn, triggered me.

"Because I can't acknowledge it!" I bellowed at her. "To acknowledge your pain, to think about what you saw, what I said to you would destroy something in me, Neera! I can't even think about what I did to you! You're my Howl! You are the last person in the world I would have hurt. I have to focus on what caused that shit and eliminate it so it's never a threat again and just not think about the pain I caused you because it would destroy me."

"You destroyed me, Night! Just because it inconveniences you to think about it, I don't have that luxury! It's right there in front of me in excruciating detail every time I close my eyes! And I saw it because you decreed I couldn't move or take my eyes off of you. I had to watch my Destined One fuck his girlfriend right in front of me. And then watch her clean your dick off with her tongue. You want to talk destroyed? You really want to talk destroyed?"

"That right there should tell you it wasn't me doing that. I would never use a decree on my Howl. I would never make you zeta. And I would never have wanted another woman once my Howl was revealed."

"And yet, you did all of that, even though you deny doing it." She sighed, and her shoulders sagged a bit. "How did you even find me? I was better off without you."

"Really, Neera? The pain you were in, the pain I was in -- it was excruciating for both of us to be apart. Your wolf was calling to my wolf in our dreams, begging us to find you. She didn't know where she was exactly, but she gave clues, as many as she could, and she kept calling out to my wolf until my trackers finally found you."

Crossing her arms over her chest, she refused to say anything. I sighed.

"Let's head back to pack lands. We can talk more when you've calmed down."

"Oh, can I ride in the front seat now? Or is it back in the trunk so I'll have even more reason to hate you?"

I hesitated too long before answering.

"Are you fucking kidding me?" she screamed -- screamed -- at me. This having a Howl business was going to take some getting used to.

"You can sit in the front seat as long as you promise not to pull any shit that could hurt you."

"Oh, thanks, daddy," she snarked at me, then went and pulled her clothes out of the trunk, having had the foresight to pull them off before she shifted.

Neera went and sat in the front seat like some sulky teenager, arms crossed over her chest, legs kicked out in front of her, head turned away from me.

And she didn't move for the next hundred and fifty miles, didn't speak. Nothing.

My phone buzzed beside me.

"Can you check the text in case it's pack business?" I asked her nicely.

She picked up my phone.

"The passcode's 63372," I told her, wondering if she'd figure it out.

She didn't say anything, just stabbed at the numbers on the screen, then sat up, rage energy pouring out of her.

"What? What's wrong?" I asked.

She tossed the phone back on the console, but I got the feeling she wanted to toss it out the window.

"Nothing's wrong. Aymeric just wanted to let you know that Lindsay Morgan's back and she's refusing to leave your house until she talks to you."

Chapter 10: So Be It

 Trigger Warning for Non-con -- Night bites Neera against her will in this chapter.*

I wanted to punch his gorgeous face so hard, then shift and rip out his throat after I read Night the text from Aymeric.

Lindsay Morgan wanted to talk with him and wasn't leaving his house until she did.

Maybe he'd drag me along for their talk and he could force me to watch them have sex again.

"We'll both talk to her, or I'll talk to her and you'll be with me."

"No, thank you. You can fuck her without an audience this time."

"Neera," he said softly, in a tone I'd never heard from him, "I'm sorry about what happened on your birthday. I am. There was more going on there than any of us knew. But I'm not really the one that hurt you. I'm not. I wouldn't have. Every fucking thing in me wants you like I've never wanted anyone in my life. I wouldn't have rejected you."

"Tell that to Lindsay Morgan," I snarled at him, then changed the subject so suddenly I'm sure he got whiplash. "I want my car back."

What I really wanted was a means of escape. I wanted to get away from him. Again.

"Two of my men arrived to get your shit from the hotel room, and they're driving your car back now." Then he looked at me from the corner of his eye. "But you won't be needing a car. You're confined to the grounds. Specifically, to my house."

Oh, hell no.

"You're stupider than I thought if you think I'm setting one foot in that house you lived in with that...bitch for three years. I have a perfectly fine apartment and that's where I'll be staying."

"Neera, there are things going on that I don't understand, but what I do understand is my instinct to protect you, and it's on full, red alert."

And then he told me about the two references to magicks Aymeric found in the ancient books, and that Raevyn was proof that at least one had survived. Her body-sharing with Blaisall was evidence that if one magick had survived and could share a body, then another one could have as well.

"We think Lindsay Morgan is body sharing, but we have no proof, so until we do, we're treating her as if we have no clue about magicks. We also think that she somehow took over my body that day, and that's why we both collapsed afterward."

"That's an awful lot of guessing and supposition based on not a lot of evidence. How convenient for you to figure out something that gets you a get out of jail free card."

"It is a lot of guessing, but it's the only theory we have that explains why in the hell I'd reject you and humiliate you. Not one other reason even comes close."

"Did you ever theorize that it's just because you're a colossal jackass and you love your long-term girlfriend?" I asked him sweetly.

"I don't love her. I never did. We think she enchanted me."

"Another convenient excuse that has no proof."

"Still the only working theory we have," Night said. "I'm not lying to you, Neera."

I didn't say anything to that, but switched the subject again. "So, what things do you and Lindsay Morgan have to discuss that are so important that she's not leaving your house?"

"No fucking clue, but Aymeric's sending her to her own apartment, even if he has to carry her. She doesn't make demands of me. If I choose to talk to her, it'll be on my terms, not hers."

"I'm still not going to your house."

He sighed like I was the biggest pain in his ass. Excellent. That was a label I could live with.

"Call Aymeric," Night said.

Seconds later, Aymeric answered, his words always more growl than voice. Owena, Echo and I always joked that even in human form, Aymeric was practically feral. It worked well for him in his role as the Alpha's Teeth. The man was beautiful...in a rabid sort of way.

"Alpha, the problem has been handled," he said, assuming Night was calling for an update.

"As I expected," he said, his praise of Aymeric probably making the man grimace. He didn't like praise, and we'd all seen his reaction when Night had, on several occasions, congratulated him publicly for handling a situation especially fast.

"Neera and I should be home in three hours or so," he said. "We need another place to stay. My Howl will not live in my house because it's contaminated."

"Probably infested with nasty-ass fleas from both of you mangy mutts," I grumped. "Maybe you could find an Alpha-sized flea collar, Aymeric. He's been scratching a lot. Probably needs a flea dip. Make sure you hold him under a good long time."

Nothing from Aymeric, who was not known for his sense of humor. Echo always said that he only got a joke if there were PowerPoints and diagrams explaining it to him. Although Aymeric didn't react, Night threw me a grin.

"You have your orders," Night said.

"No need for house hunting, Aymeric. I have my own apartment," I protested, and I heard Aymeric snort. "I'm not moving in with you, Night."

"Find us a place," Night told him. "A place that's secure for my Howl."

Silence for a moment, silence that I didn't understand but knew instinctively that I did not like.

"Understood," Aymeric said.

"Later," Night said and ended the call.

"What was that about?" I demanded. "What did you mean a place that's secure?"

"It'll be easier to show you than explain."

Three and a half hours later, I knew what Night had meant and I was ready to rip his throat out.

"There are bars on the windows," I pointed out the obvious through clenched teeth.

"Secure," Aymeric said.

"This is a solid steel door," I observed.

"Also secure."

I added Aymeric to my kill list, right under Night and Lindsay Morgan.

"Leave us," Night ordered him, and with a slight inclination of his head, Aymeric left, shutting the door behind him, closing us in the room.

Night focused those gorgeous eyes on me, and I could read the determination in them. The look sent tingles down my spine, not in a good way but in a way that raised my hackles and made me wary.

"We need to end this bullshit, Neera. You've run away from me twice now, leaving yourself exposed to our enemies. That's unacceptable to me. To make sure you're protected, we need to Take the Blood. Now. Tonight. No more waiting."

His eyes gleamed, and his wolf peered out at me. And I realized I was trapped, even more so than I had been when Night -- or whoever the hell it was -- decreed me to watch him fuck Lindsay Morgan.

I recalled the words Raevyn whispered to me before I left. Words she whispered right in my ear, her voice low, urgent and serious.

I shook my head. "No. No, we're not doing this. I rejected you, Night."

"Yes, you did, but it was only out of spite," he said, his voice dropping like all shifter males' voices did when their wolves were pushing forward. "But we're doing this, and I don't give a fuck that you rejected me. It's time to stop the bullshit. I'm your Alpha, you're my Howl, and until we Take the Blood, you're unprotected and vulnerable. That's unacceptable to me. I'm not letting you put me off any longer, Neera. I'm not going to risk you being hurt."

My heartbeat started to pick up, and I felt panic creeping in. Night stood in front of the door to the room, the damn windows had bars on them, and even if I could make it to the bathroom, Night could destroy the door in seconds, and I'd still be trapped because that window probably also had bars.

"I'm telling you no, Night," I said and...fuck my voice! It was shaky uncertain and I could not -- could not -- let this apex predator know just how scared I was. I'm sure he knew it to some extent, though, and normally that would work to my advantage because an Alpha would never want his Howl to be scared, but in a case where he thought my safety was at risk, my fear wouldn't move him. Job one for an Alpha was protecting his Howl.

If I could maneuver him to this side of the bed, I'd have to scramble over the king-sized mattress and leap for the door, hoping I could get it open before he could catch me, but I knew that was a long shot. Night was big, but he was agile and athletic and very, very fast.

"Neera, you're my Destined One, my Howl," he began, his voice throaty, coaxing me to see things from his point of view. "We're meant to be together. You ran to my house the minute you woke on your birthday because you were excited to be my Howl -- and you know if I had been in control of myself and my body that we would have Taken the Blood right then and there. Don't punish me for something I had no control over."

I swallowed, trying to think my way out of this.

"I'm not ready. I still don't trust you and I don't want this."

"Your wolf does, and she calls to me, to my wolf." He took a step toward me and I took a step back, starting to shake. "And deep down, you do, too, Neera. We were made for each other, the Forces brought us together. You're fighting your instinct. Don't fight it. Let go of your fear and stop fighting it."

His words called to me but my head fought them, fought him. In three more steps, I'd be out of room, my back against the wall, nowhere to go. Trapped.

I didn't like that feeling, and my wolf didn't either, even if she did want to be bonded to Night. She whined, feeling my panic rising. She was caught between us, her instinct to be joined with Night warring with her loyalty to me. Instinct was strong, but apparently my fear was stronger for the moment.

"Enough!" he snapped as he took another two steps toward me and I took two steps back. "You're my Howl and I need you bonded to me so I can protect you. There are bad things happening, Neera. They're concerning to me, and I don't understand them or know enough about them to know how to fight them yet. But every instinct in me is screaming that we need to Take the Blood. Now."

"Stay away from me," I held out my hands, the puniest of all defenses against this alpha male. His eyes were gleaming, his canines were lengthening and I couldn't think fast enough to stop what he was so intent on doing. "I don't want your bite, not now maybe not ever, Night. You have to trust your Destined One and I don't trust you."

"That'll change after we Take the Blood. You'll know my thoughts and I'll know yours, and you'll know you can trust me, and then I'll be able to keep you safe."

Shaking my head frantically, I felt the tears slipping from my eyes. "I'm telling you not to do it. Not now, not like this."

One shot. I had one shot to get away from him, and it was a long shot at best, but I had to try. I looked over his shoulder, widened my eyes and screamed. Night turned around, his back to me and I fucking launched myself over the bed, reaching for the door, my hand touching the handle, twisting it when his arm wrapped around my waist and he turned and threw me on the bed. His body quickly came down on mine, and he tore my shirt away from my shoulder as I sobbed and pushed against him.

He didn't give an inch.

"Don't do this. I'm begging you," I choked out, trying to twist away from him. His hand gripped my jaw, holding me in place as the tears came faster and faster. "I will never forgive you if you bite me against my will, Night. Never."

"So be it," he said, his voice guttural, his canines fully distended. "This is the only way to keep you safe."

Then his teeth ripped into that spot where my shoulder met my neck.

And I screamed.

And screamed.

And screamed.

Until he lifted his head, mouth bloody, and he tore his shirt off.

"Take my blood," he ordered me.

Raevyn's last words came to me.

Don't let him bite you. And if he does, don't bite him back. Whatever you do, do not bite him back.

Shaking and crying, feeling like I was going to throw up, I shook my head and managed to get out one word.

"No."

Chapter 11: Alpha Dreams

✱ **Trigger warning: Descriptions of violence and flashbacks to non-con bite***

When I was a young boy, my father began taking me aside and instructing me about being the Alpha -- what it meant, what my responsibilities were to the pack, to my Howl, to myself. He told me about the decrees, the strength I would have, the abilities. Once I was older and could understand the importance of keeping a secret known only by alphas and their Howls, he told me about Alpha Dreams sent to us by the Forces.

Only alphas received these dreams: they were warnings, they were advice, they were directions on how to act or the decisions to make as Alpha. Whatever their purpose was, one thing was certain...an Alpha Dream must never be ignored.

"Our dreams are given to us by the generosity of the Forces," he told me as we skipped stones on Howl Lake, one of the many lakes on Aibek pack lands. "They are gifts to us, and you must never ignore the gift they have given you, Night. Never. If you are told to act in a dream, you act. If you are told to hold back in a dream from some plans you've been making, you hold back. The dreams are never wrong. I've known some alphas of other packs who thought they knew better and ignored the warnings in a dream and it was always to their detriment."

For the last three years, I hadn't had any Alpha Dreams, and I had just chalked it up to things going well with the pack. Looking back, Lindsay Morgan had been fucking with me somehow -- the same way she'd been fucking with me to make me think I was in love with her, to make me challenge anyone who told me I shouldn't be getting so serious with someone who wasn't my Howl. The same way she'd taken over my body and caused me to reject my Howl in the worst possible way.

Since none of us knew that magic existed, we had no reason to think I was anything but in love with Lindsay Morgan, no reason to suspect I was being enchanted.

Looking back, every morning when she made me breakfast and my energy shake, she'd stroke my hair and whisper in my ear, You love me, Night, and I love you. And I'd agree.

But as soon as I separated myself from her, stopped eating the food she made me, the fog lifted from my brain, and I felt clearheaded for the first time in years. And immediately realized I had no feelings for Lindsay Morgan whatsoever.

And that was when my dreams began.

It was actually the same dream every night on repeat. I was in our family home, and four brightly wrapped boxes were brought in to me. Surrounded by the boxes, I opened the one that said OPEN ME FIRST. I ripped the paper off the box and, to my horror, inside was my mother's wolf's head, blood matting the fur where it had been ripped and torn from her body. The other boxes held the other parts of her wolf.

That had actually happened. The Luniere pack had sent first my mother and then my father back to me in pieces.

I'd thrown up, crying and shaking at the thought of my loving mother being tortured, then torn to pieces while she was still alive. My brother and I had gone berserk and had rallied our wolves to win the war between the two packs. We had been unstoppable in our fury and grief and pain.

Since then, I'd had to keep the memory pushed down inside me so I could function. The one and only Alpha Dream I'd had before Lindsay Morgan came into my life was a dream warning me not to take revenge on the Luniere pack and to keep the peace we had brokered. Originally, I'd made the pact to buy us time to find out who, specifically, was behind my parent's brutal deaths so I could exact revenge, but the Forces had spoken and I had learned the lessons well from my father. I obeyed. Unwillingly, reluctantly, but I obeyed.

But since the first time Neera had disappeared on me, the day I'd reject-ed her, I'd been having very vivid dreams of unwrapping my mother's butchered body. I looked into my mother's wolf's face, and her wolf head slowly morphed into Neera's human face. Neera's eyes popped open and her lips moved to whisper, over and over, Save me. Take my blood. Save me. Take my blood.

I awoke sweating and panting each night, realizing my Howl was out there and I had no idea where she was, which meant I couldn't protect her and we couldn't Take the Blood.

Every night that she was gone for those two weeks, the pain of being sep-arated from her was magnified by my dreams. Night after night I opened those fucking boxes, and night after night, my mother's wolf's head turned to Neera's human head and night after night she begged me to save her and take her blood.

Take her blood, the Forces were telling me.

Take her blood.

Take her blood so she didn't end up like my mother. I would protect Neera better than my father had protected my mother. For as much as he loved her, and there was no doubt about that, I always felt he had failed to protect his Howl. When I unwrapped those "gifts" containing my mother, I had resolved to do two things: win and end the war and someday, protect my Howl at all costs.

When Neera had come back after two weeks away, my wolf and I had rejoiced. Our Howl had returned, unharmed and whole, and we went tearing over to her the moment we heard she was driving onto pack lands.

My mistake was in not taking her blood right that moment when her two loyal friends stood in front of her as my wolf came racing over. I'd thought it would go over better if she could see I wasn't rejecting her, if I made the announcement in front of the pack, hoping that would undo the hurt I'd inflicted on her. But pushing me on were the two weeks of dreams: Save me. Take my blood.

The sooner I could right the wrongs I'd committed against her, the sooner we could Take the Blood and the sooner I could protect Neera. My beautiful, vulnerable, feisty Howl.

But my next mistake was agreeing to give her the night by herself. But she'd slipped out before I had my guards in place and for three terrifying weeks, the dreams had come at me again every night. Only this time, instead of whispering her pleading words to me, she was screaming them to me.

Screaming.

SAVE ME! TAKE MY BLOOD! SAVE ME! TAKE MY BLOOD!

And I knew those dreams were both warning and admonishment from the Forces that I needed to take her blood immediately when I found Neera again. I had hesitated and it had allowed Neera to escape me, leaving her wide open to...whatever evil was gathering out there.

In those three weeks, events occurred that raised my hackles. Three of our patrol wolves were found dead on the border between Aibek pack lands and Luniere pack lands. They had been gutted and their throats had been ripped out.

Then three of the Luniere patrol wolves had been found killed the same way. I met secretly with the Luniere Alpha and explained to him that my pack had not killed his wolves, and I did not think that his pack had killed my wolves. When I told him about magic and magicks and what I suspected had been going on with both Lindsay Morgan and the Raevyn, he looked shocked but said he believed me, especially when I showed him pictures on my phone of the two surviving references to the magicks from the ancient texts. Fortunately, the Forces had sent him an Alpha Dream advising him not to break the peace between our two packs.

We agreed to keep the truce, to keep our conversation between us, but to watch carefully and double patrols and be alert.

When Neera's wolf began reaching out to me in dreams during those three weeks away, I felt relief that she was still alive and we slowly were able to track her down. Throwing her into my trunk was a necessary evil in my mind. I didn't trust her not to attempt to get away, and this was the only way to assure that she came back to pack lands safely and in one piece.

I'd tried to talk her into Taking the Blood. Tried to coax her, and no matter what I'd done to her, her instinct to Take the Blood with me should have overridden everything else. It should have been impossible, but she somehow found the strength to refuse me.

Stay away from me. I don't want your bite, not now, maybe not ever, Night. You have to trust your Destined One and I don't trust you.

I'm telling you not to do it. Not now, not like this.

Don't do this. I'm begging you! I will never forgive you if you bite me against my will, Night. Never.

Being that close to me, seeing my canines lengthen, knowing we were Destined Ones should have made me irresistible to her. Everything in her should have been reaching out to me despite her feelings of pain, anger and betrayal. The instinct toward your Destined One was a force like no other and almost nothing could stop it.

Except magic.

It would explain why she was fighting me so hard.

Magic seemed like the logical answer, now that we knew about it, now that we knew what had driven me to reject her.

Save me. Take my blood.

My father's words came back to me: If you are told to act in a dream, you act.

When it came down to it, I had no choice. I had already delayed Taking her Blood and the dreams had intensified until Neera was screaming at me to do it. The Forces were guiding me as to how I should act.

So I did.

I took her blood. But my Neera refused to bite me back.

Unheard of. Once the male took his female's blood, she would take his the very second his teeth left her skin. The very second. But Neera didn't bite me back, telling me in one short word that she would not.

So now, instead of the bond forming links between us, there was only the one-way bond flowing from Neera to me. I felt her hurt, her confusion, her anger in my soul. I felt her wolf howling sadly, not understanding the lack of a return bite.

Wiping Neera's blood from my mouth with the back of my hand, I approached my Howl and she shied away from me, tears pouring from her eyes, killing me with her sorrow that I felt right down to my bones. My body was vibrating with her emotions, and I felt sick at what I'd done -- what I'd had to do -- and wanting only to make it right.

Neera, back against the wall, slowly slid down it until she was sitting on the floor, knees up, her shoulder bleeding. Then she crossed her arms over her knees and put her head down on them. Sobs wracked her body, that little form shaking as if her world had ended.

My wolf whined several times, and I paced in front of Neera, unsure of how to proceed. How did I fix this? How did I make her understand why I'd bitten her against her will? I wanted to explain to her about the Alpha Dreams, about the wolves killed from the two packs, about the magic my brother, Aymeric and I feared was at play. Would she listen now? Should I wait for morning?

Save me. Take my blood. SAVE ME! TAKE MY BLOOD!

My wolf whined and whined, not liking the sight of Neera in tears, and I finally let him out when I realized I wasn't making any progress with her. After watching her for a long moment, he dropped to his belly and crawled over to her, desperate to stop her pain but not knowing how to. Whining softly, he eventually began lapping at her wound, cleaning her blood and helping to heal her mark.

She startled at the first pass of his tongue on her shoulder, but then dropped her head back on her arms. When her wound was cleaned, my wolf sat pressed beside her, keeping vigil as she cried.

We stayed like that almost the entire night. When Neera finally passed out from exhaustion, I shifted back, picked her up and held her in my arms until morning.

Chapter 12: We Were In Trouble

I remembered my sister's words when I saw her three weeks ago: Soon, Ifrita. Soon.

Soon we would finish what we had started many, many years ago with the other magicks, but the wolves had miraculously stopped. Somehow those mangy mutants had discovered what was going on and had destroyed our people instead of us destroying them.

As it should have been.

Although those vile hairballs had learned how to stop the magicks, Raevyn and I had later snuck in and destroyed the evidence in the wolves' archives, leaving nothing behind that hinted at magicks. We erased all knowledge not only of us, but of how to destroy us. That would be critical for the plans my sister and I had.

Then we sat back and bided our time, patiently waiting for hundreds of years until the memory of magic and the magicks faded...and faded some more until it was a hazy, vague memory...and finally was forgotten altogether.

Three years ago, following the war between the Aibek pack and the Luniere pack, which my sister and I helped to start, I discarded the body I had claimed at the last moment when Raevyn and I were about to be killed all those centuries ago.

Blaisall had become sufficiently cowed with my sister running her body, knowing the nasty consequences of disobeying my sister's wishes, but the woman's body I had taken four hundred years ago still, even after all this time, tried to assert herself. Dalela needed to die.

So I found Lindsay Morgan, the weakest woman ever. She and her Destined One had just discovered each other when I appeared, and when presented with a choice between her Destined One's life and her own, she chose her own. I left Dalela's body -- which, now that it was four hundred years old and without its magick, quickly crumbled into dust. Bye bye, Dalela. It's been fun.

Lindsay Morgan's body was much easier to control since she had already proven her innate weakness. She stayed down, down, down, never trying to surface, and I was able to enchant Night with a drink I kindly brought to my Alpha and a few words whispered into his ear. He became mine, never suspecting he was under enchantment because all knowledge of magic had been erased from the wolves. How can you suspect something that doesn't exist? He thought he'd been struck by love, the fool, but I made sure to whisper those words into his ear each morning and each night as he drank my special concoction.

You love me, Night, and I love you.

Very little magic could be performed without some sort of concoction, and if it was, it could drain a magick quickly.

The day Neera showed up at our door, I knew we were in trouble and our plans were at risk. I had answered the door before I could make Night's concoction and whisper the spell into his ear, never thinking it would be his motherfucking Howl.

He'd started to look at her, so I quickly turned Night's head and took over his body, making him drag her to the Den. That had been hard enough, so I receded from him, thinking I could save some of my strength, but damned if he didn't look at her again. I could almost see the bond starting to form between them, so I surged back into him, long enough to ensure Neera was thoroughly, completely and totally rejected and humiliated.

That half hour had drained me, drained him and we both collapsed.

After I regained consciousness, I got word to my sister. I knew Night wouldn't let me near him again, the Alpha not knowing what was afoot, only that something was. If I couldn't get near to him, I couldn't spell him. He refused to see me, try as I might to get him back to me.

It would be up to Raevyn. She got word to me when Neera was leaving her place, saying only that she had fed Neera concoctions every day for two weeks and had spelled her right when she left with a particularly strong spell, hoping that it would prevent her from accepting Night's bite for a few months.

Long enough to buy us some time.

Long enough to put our plans in motion.

Long enough to start another war and help the wolves to destroy each other. Then we could move on to the next two packs, until eventually, someday, all of the wolves would be dead and we would have vengeance for what the wolves had done to our own kind.

When Neera ran from him almost immediately upon her return from my sister, I couldn't believe our luck.

So in the time she was gone, I was able to kill Aibek wolves and make it look like the Luniere pack had committed the crime; then I framed the Aibek pack for the deaths of the Luniere wolves.

Then Night had found Neera and brought her back. Rumors this morning said he had Taken her Blood, but she had not returned the favor.

Thank you, Raevyn.

Her magic had held, fortunately. It was already difficult enough to destroy so many mutts; but a Bonded wolf was another creature entirely and in this way the wolves had almost ended the magicks completely four hundred years ago. Even our small bursts of magic couldn't stop a Bonded wolf for long, and the wolf would recover before we could. If Night and Neera completed the Taking of the Blood, that would mean the end of Raevyn and me.

We could not let Neera Take his Blood, or all of our years of waiting, all of the years of planning and moving the pieces into place, would be for nothing.

Now that she was back, but not fully his Howl, I would need to act fast, in case my sister's spell failed and Neera wanted to bite him back. Complete the bond.

Neera Karis needed to cease existing.

And I was just the magick to make sure it happened.

Brutally.

If I could do it right in front of Night's eyes, so much the better because I knew the pain it would cause him. He'd certainly cried like a little bitch when his mother came back to him in pieces. He never realized he'd been sleeping with his mother's killer for three years. It made me laugh inside every time I made him tell me he loved me.

Now, when I ended his Howl, I would savor his pain in person.

Right before I ended him, too.

This was going to be so delicious, especially after waiting so many long, frustrating years.

All I needed was for Raevyn to arrive and then we could execute our plan.

And end the two packs, once and for all.

Chapter 13: I'm Protecting You

Alphas are all about being over the top. They have more confidence than fifty men. They're huge compared to almost all other men, as both human and wolf. They're faster than other men, no contest. They're utterly assured and in control in all situations. In fact, the more threatening the situation, the better they are. They thrive on being challenged, being in charge and caring for their pack members.

And in cases where they've fucked up with their mates, they're the biggest babies in the world.

Sad eyes? The very saddest and droopiest.

Hang dog look? The hang doggiest.

Pathetic? The most pitiful in the world.

The morning after Night bit me against my will, I slowly came awake in his arms. I last remembered crying on the floor, my back against the wall, Night's monster wolf huddled beside me. I'd almost jumped out of my skin when I'd first felt the lick of his wolf's tongue against my bite mark, then quickly settled down as he continued his healing ministrations on my mark.

The bite mark I hadn't wanted.

Had refused, in fact. Several times.

But not much other than a bigger, scarier force of nature could stop an Alpha wolf from Taking the Blood with his Destined One. And even then, the Alpha wolf would fight to his death to get through whatever was keeping him from his Howl. It was part of our most basic natures, a biological imperative that could not be denied. An Alpha could not resist his Howl, and vice versa.

So how had I denied him? How had I fought and protested the bite? Nothing should have stopped me, not even Raevyn's words of warning to me not to let Night bite me, and if he did, to not bite him back.

Thinking back to the morning of my twenty-first birthday, I thought about how happy I'd been when I looked in the mirror and realized I was the Howl. My Destined One was known to me -- I wouldn't have to wait for the Forces to bring us together since I knew exactly where to find him. On my run over to Night's house, I'd been planning our future and children together. Of course he'd give up Lindsay Morgan now that his Destined One was revealed. He'd have no other choice. In a word, I would be irresistible to him.

Or I should have been impossible to resist.

Now, after the pain of him rejecting me, then me rejecting him, through the pain of running away from my Destined One not once, but twice, through the helplessness of him Taking my Blood without my consent, I was waking up, cradled in his arms. He was sitting on the floor, clearly having taken my place there, his back against the wall, and his eyes were on me.

Focused on me with startling intensity.

After behaving so horribly to me, after biting me without my consent, he'd held me all night long and I'd slept in his arms peacefully, like a baby. I'd fucking slept in the arms of the man who had Taken my Blood against my will.

Not liking what that implied, with a yelp, I jumped out of his arms, too fast for even his amazing reflexes to stop me and I quickly put the bed between us. Slowly, carefully, not making any fast moves, he got to his feet, not wanting to freak me out any more than I was.

"Neera, we need to talk," he said calmly, making no move to pursue me as he had last night. Would I be safe over here?

Don't think about that.

"I'm not going to come after you, so yes, you're safe over there. I know you're scared of me right now, but I need to tell you about things that have been happening, about magic, about some recent deaths in our pack and the Luniere pack, about why I Took your Blood last night without your permission."

OK, that one sentence alone could take a while to unpack. Of course, my mind focused on the most inane thing out of all of that he'd said.

"How did you know I was worried about being safe over here?"

"Because I know your thoughts now. Apparently, even though our bond is half-formed, it still allows me to hear what you're thinking. You can't get my feelings yet, and you won't until you Take my Blood."

"Well, don't hold your breath on that happening after what you put me through last night."

The look on his face. Total hang dog. He was devastated, and his wolf even whined a bit, enough for me to hear. No male would ever hurt his female, and what Night had done to me was about the worst thing a Destined One could do to his other half. What was supposed to be a beautiful moment filled with desire and longing had been sheer terror for me.

"I'm sorry, Neera, I'm so sorry you were terrified of me, but I did what I had to do, and you'd understand if you'd listen."

Seriously? This apology was right up there with his inability to think about his brutal rejection of me because it would cause him pain.

"I'm sorry for that, too," he said, reading my thoughts once again. This could be really problematic. "I'll try to apologize for it, but it really wasn't my fault --"

This again!

"You rejected me, Night. You rejected me by screwing Lindsay Morgan, a three-year girlfriend of yours that you shouldn't even have had. And you can't even say sorry for letting your dick follow the yellow brick road to Lindsay's Munchkinland -- right in front of me no less? And just to say, the guys I've been with lasted a lot longer than you did with Lindsay."

"Were they in our pack?"

"What?"

"The guys you were with," he growled at me, or his wolf did. "Were. They. In. Our. Pack?"

"As if I'd tell you," I scoffed at him, trying not to think of the two guys I'd dated from the Luniere pack when I was eighteen and nineteen.

Obviously forgetting, once again, that one of us could read the other's thoughts.

"Perfect. I'll ask around and have a chat so they know there won't be any future with you. And to steer clear of me if I ever have reason to enter Luniere pack lands. You won't be going to their lands ever again."

"Seriously, Night? But it's OK that you had a live-in girlfriend for three years and then you rejected me?"

"That wasn't me doing it," he said, trying to remain calm but I could see his nose twitching and his canines lengthening. "And stay away from Lindsay. I don't want you anywhere near her."

"Oh, my Forces! You're protecting her now?"

"No, I'm protecting you," he said, and his voice was guttural, as if he was fighting the shift. "She's one of the things we need to talk about. I don't want you near her because she's dangerous, we think."

And then he proceeded to explain about the scraps of paper they found about magic and the magicks in the ancient texts, about the deaths of both Aibek and Luniere pack members, about what they suspected had happened over the last three years with Lindsay Morgan enchanting Night and using her magic to take control of his body and words the day he'd rejected me. He also told me about the Alpha Dreams he'd been having, after cautioning me not to tell anyone about the sacred visions sent by the Forces.

"All that said, I'm sorry about the misunderstandings, but again, it wasn't me doing any of that. I couldn't have resisted you had I been in control of my senses. Everything about you reaches out to me, Neera, like a siren's song. You're mine, into eternity, and I want you to Take the Blood, now, so I can protect you."

Swallowing, I shook my head. "I can't."

At my words, Night snarled at me, one hundred percent pissed off Alpha who wasn't being obeyed.

"I need to protect you; this is the only way." Then he thought a minute. "Is this about the trunk thing?"

"The trunk -- oh, you mean when you kidnapped me?"

"I didn't kidnap you," he protested firmly.

"What would you call throwing someone in your trunk against her will?"

"I relocated you. From the hotel to pack lands, where --"

"Once again, against my will, so by definition, it's a kidnapping!"

"I needed to protect you!" he shouted at me. "And you need to bite me, right now, so I can protect you as an Alpha protects his Howl."

Try as I might, I could not bring myself to do it. My canines weren't lengthening and without those, I couldn't bite him. Something must be holding me back for a reason.

Night cocked his head, trying to puzzle out my refusal. "Let's go for a run," he finally suggested. "That will help you clear your head and think logically. We'll let our wolves out to play and then talk some more afterward."

No. If I let my wolf out, she'd bite him in a heartbeat. I might not have the desire to bite him, but she was practically forcing herself out of me to get at him. Night and his wolf were everything a fur-girl could want, strong, handsome and supremely Alpha, and she wanted more than anything to complete the bond.

But no way was I going to let that happen without my consent this time. Night took the control out of my hands last night and I wasn't ready to let that go, whatever his reasons. He would just have to wait until I had the desire to complete the bond and Take his Blood.

Suddenly smiling, Night pushed and I realized -- too late, once again -- that the man could hear my thoughts. "Good to know one of you is in your right mind. Let her out, Neera. Just let her out to play."

If seduction had a voice, it would be Night's -- low and deep, coaxing, raspy with desire and want. Need.

Even though he hadn't taken a step toward me, I backed away. "Stop it! I said no, and this time I hope you'll honor my wishes instead of doing something against my will."

He looked like I'd slapped him, his eyes immediately stricken, his wolf peeping through mournfully. Hang dog expression in place.

See? Pathetic and pitiful.

"I'll give you until tonight," he said, as if he were a king granting me a boon, "but it will happen before the day is over. In the meantime, Aymeric will be with you every moment."

He stepped past me and opened the door, and called for Aymeric, giving him strict instructions.

"I'm hungry," I snapped at him as Night started to walk off.

"Aymeric will take you to the Den for breakfast. Eat and drink only what he hands you himself."

Snapping a salute at him, I agreed to follow that rule.

Ten minutes later, as Aymeric was walking me to the Den, Lindsay Morgan came toward me with her two sidekicks, Cindy and Courtney, and blocked our path. Aymeric told her to move, but she held her ground.

"I need to say something quick to Neera," she told him. "And sweetie, I just wanted to say, you're welcome to my leftovers. But be with him knowing that he loved me for three years, he fucked me for three years, and he rejected you for me. So maybe you have the Alpha-Howl vibe going, but it's only because of the bond. Not because he truly cares for you. I'm the one he loves. You may be his Destined One, but you'll never be the one he l oves."

With a last look at me, she walked away, her two minions following, all of them laughing softly as they distanced themselves from me.

Aymeric shot me a look, then motioned toward the Den, where I ran into Owena and Echo. We hugged and talked and ate breakfast together, and I filled them in on how I'd come to be back on pack lands (they agreed I'd been kidnapped) and how Night had Taken my Blood against my will. Echo looked like she was about to cry when I told her that and Owena, surprisingly, looked like she wanted to join her.

We talked for almost two hours, catching up on the last three weeks before Aymeric grunted that it was time to go.

"Good chatting with you, Meri," Echo taunted him as she got up from the table. "Next time let a girl get a word in edgewise."

He bared his teeth at her but otherwise said nothing. With a wave, she and Owena walked away and Aymeric took me back to my prison.

We walked into the house, and when he closed and locked the door behind us, Lindsay Morgan and Raevyn appeared from the hallway.

Before Aymeric or I could move or react, Lindsay Morgan had blown a light purple powder at both of us from the palm of her hand, right into our faces.

"Sleep," Raevyn intoned as Lindsay kept blowing the powder at us. "Sleep deep. Sleep."

I don't know which one of us hit the floor first.

Chapter 14: Shift!

✱ **Trigger warning for violent acts being discussed.***

I'd left Neera with Aymeric while I went to handle some pack business with Néron. After devoting my morning to the pack, I could be with my Howl for the remainder of the day, working to get her to a point that she was willing to Take my Blood. That was critical, and I was baffled as to why, now that she knew everything, she was still unwilling to bite me.

He's an idiot if he thinks some vague explanations about magic are enough for me to forget that rejection of me.

I grunted as I heard Neera's thoughts and missed the question my brother had asked me about the Luniere pack. Their Alpha wanted to meet with me to discuss some other strange happenings. Unfortunately, all I could think about was tracking down Neera and showing her just how much of an idiot I was.

I shot a quick text to Aymeric.

All good?

As usual, his wordy reply took forever to read:

Yes

I sighed. Every fucking time. The Alpha's Teeth could never give more information or expand on his answers unless asked specific questions.

Are you still at the Den?

His response came quickly:

Yes

Pinching the bridge of my nose, I typed out another text:

Who's with her?

His response wasn't as swift this time, and I almost choked when I read his answer:

Owena. And that Echo who is a mouthy little wolf begging for discipline over my knee to fix her attitude

Well, fuck if that wasn't interesting. My Alpha's Teeth saw women as a nuisance and had always claimed he was content to be single, happy that so far the Forces had not sent him a Destined One. I strongly suspected he'd never fucked a woman or he might not find them so objectionable. It was all about the job with Aymeric, and he took his position as my Alpha's Teeth seriously. That he wanted to put that little wolf over his knee spoke volumes to me. I assumed she was slightly younger than Neera, so her mate brand hadn't appeared yet.

To put Aymeric's tail in a twist, I texted back:

As my Alpha's Teeth, you're in charge of pack discipline, so if she needs some, feel free

Three dots appeared and then disappeared for an entire minute.

She's going to get a bare-ass spanking if she doesn't stop

I burst out laughing.

The type of discipline is at your discretion. I don't need or want details

This time, it took two minutes for him to reply.

She makes my dick hard and I don't know what to do about it since that hasn't happened before

Oh, for fuck's sake. He and my brother were my closest friends, but I did not want to know this shit. I'd be willing to bet my father hadn't dealt with this type of shit from his Alpha's Teeth. Still, he was a pack member and he seemed to be asking for my advice. Cringing, I typed out a response.

Ask her out on a date or ask if she's DTF but I don't want to hear any more details

Tell him if she smells good to lick her face, my wolf interjected.

OK, enough of this bullshit was enough. I needed to finish up pack business so I could get to my Howl and talk her into Taking my Blood. I needed this bond to go both ways so we could communicate. I'd feel much better, given the uncertainty of things right now. Lindsay Morgan was still moving about at will, although I had eyes on her; I was unwilling to imprison the bitch since I didn't know what she was capable of with her magic. I wanted her to go on thinking we had no idea what she was until I had more information and was ready to move on her.

Tell him, my wolf scratched at me in such a way I knew he wouldn't shut the fuck up until I gave Aymeric some wolf advice. With another sigh, I typed out what I hoped to the Forces would be the last text on the subject.

My wolf said if she smells good, lick her face

The reply came back fast:

I like it so I'm going to try it

Needing some sanity in my life, I texted the group of Lindsay Morgan watchers.

Report

Four replies were almost instantaneous:

Quiet

Nothing happening

All good

No problems

Right before I finished the last of my paperwork, Aymeric texted to say he and Neera were heading back to the secure house.

Tell me when you get there

After I finished up my paperwork, some pack members came in with a minor disagreement they needed me to arbitrate, so I listened and told them my solution. Once they agreed to the terms I set out, I checked my phone to see half an hour had passed...and there had been no text from Aymeric. Irritated, I texted him.

You at the house yet?

No dots, even after a minute. That was odd. Aymeric always responded to me within seconds. Feeling for my connection to Neera, I was disconcerted to find there was nothing. Not even a stray thought to read.

Shit.

Concerned that something was wrong, I ran to Néron's office, and he shot to his feet when he saw the look on my face.

"What's wrong, brother?"

"I don't know that anything's wrong, but Aymeric hasn't texted me to say he and Neera were safely back at the secure house. And he didn't respond just now to another text."

"Shit," Néron said, and with a glance at each other, we were both out the door, running flat out for the secure house, just over the next hill.

What the hell was going on? Come on, give me some clues if you can, Neera. Then I felt it, weak and thready, but there.

Night.

I waited as we continued running for the house.

Help.

I wished once again she had completed the Taking of the Blood so she could read my thoughts and she'd know exactly what I wanted to know -- needed to know.

Tell me where you are, I pleaded uselessly, knowing she couldn't hear my thoughts. What's going on?

The house was just ahead of us.

Tell me where you are, Neera. Tell me where they've taken you!

Lindsay. Raevyn. Prison.

Prison? It didn't dawn on me what she meant until Néron and I burst through the door of the secure house, ready to start tracking Neera down, when we realized we didn't have to.

"Shut the door," a woman I assumed was the Raevyn ordered me, and I obeyed since Lindsay Morgan had Neera's back against her front, and a wicked looking knife pricking my Howl's throat, a steady stream of blood trickling down her neck. Raevyn stood right next to Lindsay Morgan.

"Lovely to finally meet you on the day you're going to die," Raevyn drawled.

I said nothing, and I could feel Néron tense beside me. From the corner of my eyes, I saw Aymeric tied up and bleeding in the corner. He was still alive.

"This day has been a long time coming, since four hundred years ago when a wolf killed a magick simply because he'd killed the wolf's mate, and that began an all-out war between the magicks and the wolves. Your kind eventually figured out how to destroy us, and my sister and I were the last ones left alive, about to be killed, when we saved ourselves."

Lindsay jumped in. "We had to wait for the memories to fade, to lay low until it was time to rise and finish the work we'd begun all those centuries ago. Since your pack and the Luniere pack began it all, we thought we'd start with you."

"That's fine," I told the sisters. "Start with me, but let Neera go. We'll do a trade."

Lindsay laughed. "I think not. You wolves aren't getting out of here alive. It just depends on the order you go out in."

"Oh, Ifrita, I just can't decide how this should go," Raevyn said.

"I want to start with the bitch. The only question is, should I hack Neera into pieces as a human or a wolf?" Lindsay asked Raevyn before turning her attention back to me. "Killing your parents as wolves was fun, but I'm thinking carving up a human might be even more fun because that way we can all hear her begging. Unfortunately, with your parents they could only whine and howl in pain since we spelled them to prevent them from shifting back into humans. Sometimes they whimpered, poor, pathetic pooches. I must say, watching your father trying to get to your mother as we ripped her apart was so very entertaining."

"It'd been years since we laughed that hard," Raevyn said with a fond smile of remembrance.

Don't react. I forced myself to ignore their words and concentrate on a plan. If we survived this, Néron and I would have plenty of time to work out the pain of hearing about our parents' last moments. I could feel my little brother forcing himself to be calm beside me, and I wished I could offer him comfort. Neera's thoughts had gone silent since I entered the house.

Think. What was it Echo had said Blaisall told them about Raevyn? When my wolf is out, her magic doesn't work.

The plan that began forming in my mind was risky, no doubt, but it was all I could think of, weak though it was. I'd know exactly what to do if I had been up against wolves, but I was faced with not one but two magicks, and I had no idea what they were capable of, what kind of destruction they could rain down on us.

These two women hated wolves and planned to kill all of us. If they started with the four of us in this room, the pack was fucked. Aymeric, Néron and I were the three strongest wolves in the pack, and I had no confidence that the other sub-alphas could figure out how to defeat the two magicks since they had no idea they even existed or what they were.

I was an Alpha without his Howl, which left us without the incredible power of the Bonded Wolf. My plan continued to take shape as I listened to Raevyn and Lindsay Morgan talk without paying attention to what they were saying. Formulating a do-or-die plan was taking all my concentration, but I hated that it depended on if and might.

If this happens...

If that also happens...

Then it might work...

If was a very risky gamble with Neera's life, all of our lives, hanging in the balance. The very future of the entire pack depended on this if and might plan working.

Weak, but I had no other options.

If and might were all I had right now, in addition to split second timing, followed closely by I hope Néron can figure out in less than a second what I need him to do.

Solid motherfucking plan.

I can't let my wolf out. She wants to bite you. Take the Blood.

I prayed to the Forces that what Neera's thoughts had told me about her wolf's overwhelming desire was still true.

Without appearing to, I focused and gathered myself, drawing on all of my Alpha strength and power, hoping it would be enough to do what I needed to get done.

Not knowing if it would work on wolves who had been ruthlessly repressed for so long by the magicks. Needing it to happen with all four at the exact same moment. I couldn't even look at Neera's face for fear of losing my focus.

Split second timing...

If...

If...

Might...

"Maybe I'll start hacking pieces off Neera's pretty little neck to start," Lindsay Morgan's words drew my attention, and she began sawing the knife deeper into Neera's neck as the evil bitch smiled right at me.

I was out of time. I had to act. No time for second-guessing.

With that realization, I bellowed an Alpha Decree, my muscles straining with the force of the power and command I threw behind the single word:

Chapter 15: Dropped

****Trigger warning for acts of violence*****

I felt as if I'd been in a deep sleep and my alarm had blasted me awake leaving me groggy, slow-moving and dazed. Strangely dazed, to the point that my muscles didn't want to cooperate and I couldn't get my legs under me.

A sharp slap on my face woke me up faster. Bits and pieces were slowly coming back to me.

Leaving the Den.

Walking into the house.

Something else, something sinister teased the edge of my consciousness...

Raevyn and Lindsay Morgan.

Another sharp slap and a kick to my stomach made the rest of my brain fog dissipate, and I struggled to sit up. Before I could, Lindsay Morgan kicked me in the chest so hard I couldn't breathe right, and I desperately tried to pull air into my lungs, gasping and choking, as I tried to recall that last piece of the puzzle --

Lindsay Morgan blowing powder in our faces and Raevyn telling us to sleep.

And then, nothing.

Aymeric! My gaze searched for and found him on the floor, across the room from me.

Unlike me, he'd been bound with heavy chains, tightly, like a mummy, so I knew he wasn't going anywhere soon. Worrying about the puddle of blood slowly and steadily spreading beneath his head, I tried to gather my wits...until the tip of Lindsay Morgan's shoe caught me under the chin, throwing me back down onto the floor.

Looking up, she stood over me, smiling such a sweet smile that I knew she was completely fucking psychotic and was going to kill us.

And enjoy it.

"If you shift, we'll kill Aymeric and then we'll kill you. Now, call him to you," she demanded.

There was no doubt him was referring to Night. "Give me a phone and I will," I lied, trying to buy more time. Trying to think.

BAM!

Wrong thing to say and she caught me in the stomach that time with her foot. Then for good measure, she grabbed a handful of my hair and slammed my face into the floor.

"I see your bite mark," she hissed into my face. "He Took your Blood, which means he can hear your thoughts so do not fuck with me," she warned.

Little did she know that I probably had already revealed too much when I'd awakened and was scrambling to figure out what was going on and pull my thoughts together. His name had been in my mind.

Night.

Then when I'd seen Aymeric bleeding on the floor, I'd thought, Help.

Wanting to warn him, I'd told him that Lindsay and Raevyn were at the prison house, as I thought of the place. He'd know. He'd told me what he suspected, and I hoped and prayed to the Forces he could figure out a way to stop them before we lost any more of the pack.

Maybe my thoughts would be enough to warn him, to help him formulate a plan to save the pack. I had a chilling feeling it was too late for Aymeric and me. The puddle of blood under the Alpha's Teeth continued to pool at an alarming rate.

Raevyn lifted her head, watching out the window. "He's a fool, just like his father, thinking he can save his Howl. This should be entertaining."

Before I could warn him not to come in, Night and Néron burst through the door of the house and came to a stop, just after Lindsay Morgan had pulled me to my feet and pressed a wicked-looking knife to my neck. I forced my mind to be quiet, to not panic, to go blank so Night wouldn't get any distracting thoughts from me.

I knew, Alpha that he was, he was already working on how to get us out of this, and he'd be more than willing to die trying if it meant saving me.

"Shut the door," Raevyn ordered him, and Night did as she asked, buying himself, and all of us, time.

"Lovely to finally meet you on the day you're going to die," Raevyn taunted him. "This day has been a long time coming, since four hundred years ago when a wolf killed a magick simply because he'd killed the wolf's mate, and that began an all-out war between the magicks and the wolves. Your kind eventually figured out how to destroy us, and my sister and I were the last ones left alive, about to be killed, when we saved ourselves."

Lindsay continued the story none of us knew. "We had to wait for the memories to fade, to lay low until it was time to rise and finish the work we'd begun all those centuries ago. Since your pack and the Luniere pack began it all, we thought we'd start with you."

"That's fine," Night said, though his voice was guttural. That meant his wolf was near the surface and Night was fighting his instinct to shift, but he was managing to sound as agreeable as an Alpha wolf could when his Howl was threatened. "Start with me, but let Neera go. We'll do a trade."

Lindsay laughed, digging the knife a little deeper into my neck, and I could feel the blood flowing from the cut. "I think not. You wolves aren't getting out of here alive. It just depends on the order you go out in."

"Oh, Ifrita, I just can't decide how this should go," Raevyn pretended to enjoy contemplating her choices.

"I want to start with the bitch. The only question is, should I hack Neera into pieces as a human or a wolf?" Ifrita asked.

Then she spoke directly to Night, and what she said broke my heart, making it almost impossible to not shift in my rage.

"Killing your parents as wolves was fun, but I'm thinking carving up a human might be even more fun because that way we can all hear her begging. Unfortunately, with your parents they could only whine and howl in pain since we spelled them to prevent them from shifting back into humans. Sometimes they whimpered, poor, pathetic pooches. I must say, watching your father trying to get to your mother as we ripped her apart was so very entertaining," Ifrita said as calmly as if she'd been discussing a new recipe.

Night had held his body perfectly still as Lindsay Morgan -- Ifrita -- taunted him about killing his parents, but he showed no outward sign of emotion.

Raevyn looked at Néron and Night.

"Now, make sure you don't shift for the next part of the story, or we'll be forced to end things much more quickly than planned. Just think of it as telling you a bedtime story. We know you always wondered how we got your mother and it was actually quite simple. We set a trap for her in the woods, saying we had captured her sons and if she wanted to see you alive ever again, she would come immediately. On the note was a special powder that blocked her bond with your father. She ran to save you boys while your father was taking care of pack war business with his Alpha's Teeth. We followed your mother into the woods and used the sleeping powder on her, then took her to a special little house we had, not too far from here," Raevyn explained.

Ifrita continued the horrible narrative. "We spelled your mother to prevent her from shifting and chained her to the ground so she could barely move. Then we used some more of that wonderful sleeping powder on her so she couldn't reach out to your father before we bagged his ass. The next day, we came back for your father and lured him to us by pretending to be members of the Luniere pack with information about his Howl. Well, we did have information about his Howl, so that part was true. A little bit of the sleeping powder and...he was sleeping like a baby. Big fucking wolf, just like you two. It was hard to wrap him in chains and get him in the trunk. But we managed, you'll be relieved to know, and we spelled him, too, to make sure he couldn't shift to human."

Night still had shown no reaction, and I wondered if he was tuning her out so he could focus on trying to get us out of this mess. I could tell his lack of reaction infuriated both Ifrita and Raevyn, so they continued hammering at him with the horrifying details of his parents' deaths. At this point, I was more concerned with Néron shifting; I could see him vibrating with rage, his fingers twitching, but so far, he was holding back his wolf.

"Once we got your father into the house," Raevyn said, "we chained him inside so he could watch through the window while we...played with your mother, so to speak."

"Such fun to watch her writhe and howl in pain -- and when we started dismantling her...well, I don't know if it was more fun watching your father's useless, frantic attempts to get to her or watching her agony until we finally took her head," Ifrita added happily.

The sisters laughed in delight at the shared memory, proving their crazy went deep, all the way to the bone.

"It was a good day, sister, and now we get to have the same kind of fun again," Ifrita said to Raevyn. "Maybe I'll start hacking pieces off Neera's pretty little neck to start."

With that, she began sawing the knife deeper into my neck, and it went deep.

Pressing my lips together, I refused to whimper or acknowledge the pain, realizing we were running out of time. I was going to die, and it wouldn't be pretty or painless, but I refused to let these bitches see me cower or beg for mercy.

With Ifrita's words and actions, Night's body tensed, his muscles straining though he wasn't moving one bit, the veins standing out on his arms, in his neck. His face was composed, almost as if he was bored, separated from the things happening right in front of him, distant from the words they were throwing at him, hoping to spark a reaction.

And suddenly, without warning, Night bellowed the loudest, strongest, most commanding Alpha Decree I'd ever heard in my life to shift. So forceful, I wouldn't be surprised if pack members all over Aibek lands suddenly started shifting without knowing why.

My wolf came forward instantly and fucking launched herself at Night's shoulder where she bit him, finally Taking his Blood, then he yelled, "As One!" and for the first time ever, Night and I merged to form our massive Bonded Wolf.

I'd heard a Bonded Wolf was enormous, but our wolf was beyond huge. We dwarfed Néron's wolf by a good two feet at the shoulder, our paws practically the size of dinner plates.

Now we were facing Ifrita, who was obviously fighting Lindsay Morgan's wolf for control. The poor wolf was trying to come forward and obey the Alpha Decree. Raevyn was likewise fighting to suppress Blaisall's wolf.

Néron had shifted and his normally giant wolf seemed dwarfed beside us as he waited to act.

They need to shift for this to work. Everything depends on them shifting. Everything. They must shift!

I could hear Night's thoughts now. Then we gave a sharp, deep bark -- the wolf version of the Alpha Decree to SHIFT!

For a few seconds, the longest seconds of my life, I watched as the battle between the magicks and the wolves was fought.

And won by the wolves.

The wolves stood before us, which meant the magicks were suppressed, and oddly, the two wolves immediately lifted their heads up, as if they were going to howl, exposing their necks.

At once, Néron leapt for Blaisall's wolf and we threw ourself at Lindsay Morgan's wolf.

Our teeth gripped the wolf's throat and we bit down as we yanked our head back, tearing the wolf's throat out in one sharp, swift movement. Néron did the same thing to Blaisall's wolf's throat.

The two wolves dropped to the floor where they stood.

The magicks inside them as dead as the wolves.

In ten seconds, start to finish, it had ended.

Four hundred years after it began, the wolves had finished the war with the magicks.

Chapter 16: They Knew The Gesture

In the aftermath of an intense, life-or-death situation, once everything is over, there is a surreal calm that surrounds you, making you question if you had, in fact, lived through something that extreme where your life hung in the balance. This calm blankets you, maybe to temporarily soften the sharp edges of the experience, giving you some space to catch your breath before you have to face what happened and start processing the event.

It was the morning after we'd killed the magicks, and I was walking toward the lake as the sun rose, reflecting orange and pink on the water. From here, I could see my Howl sitting on the shore, her knees pulled up, arms wrapped around her legs, her head resting on her knees. I hated seeing her in that position, hated that it reminded me of the position she'd been in after I'd Taken her Blood.

She was clearly in the processing stage after yesterday, but I resisted reaching out through our bond. Not invading her thoughts at the moment so she could have some privacy, some time to herself, seemed like the least I could do for her.

My little Howl had been to hell and back since her birthday, and yesterday alone was mind fuck enough, never mind everything else she'd endured.

Yesterday had been too close, way too close in timing, in the plan just not working.

Néron and my Neera -- and Aymeric, despite being unconscious -- had shifted immediately at my Alpha Decree. Ifrita and Raevyn, realizing that I'd commanded all wolves in the room in such a way that they had no choice but to obey, had tried to prevent the wolves inside their bodies from coming forward.

As Neera Took my Blood, I watched as the magicks fought the wolves and realized this could easily go the other way, in a direction that was decidedly not in our favor.

Neera and I formed our Bonded Wolf and we waited beside Néron's wolf, vibrating with tension and energy, then we barked another Alpha Decree, hoping that might shift the balance of power, hoping the two wolves would come forward even if just for a second. That was all the time we needed -- and all the time we might have before Ifrita and Raevyn were able to surge forward and suppress them again.

Not knowing how long the magicks would stay down if the wolves won, we had to be ready to move instantly.

And we did, the very second the wolves shifted forward -- and bared their necks to us -- we fucking moved, killing them in less than three seconds after they shifted.

We'd finished the war, and had the bodies and throats at our feet to prove it. As soon as we had spit out the grisly mess in our mouths, we shifted back, and I grabbed Neera as she stumbled.

My Howl was a mess, bleeding and bruised, clearly having been beaten by the magicks before I'd arrived. I would have given anything to keep those magicks alive and torture them for months just for what they'd done to my Howl alone. But knowing what those bitches had done to my parents? I only wished I could have prolonged their deaths, visiting on them what they had done to my mother and father...but much more slowly and painfully, drawing it out until they were begging for death, and even then, I'd keep the torture going until all that was left to torture was just a puddle of blood.

"I'm OK. I'm OK," Neera kept repeating as we joined Néron, who was now crouched by Aymeric. My call to shift had been strong enough to call his wolf forward, but he'd become entangled in the chains. Néron and I quickly dealt with those, looking for the wound that had caused all the blood. There were two deep slices on each side of his neck that, though serious, had fortunately missed his arteries.

I'd called on my phone for the pack doctors, who swiftly came and stitched him up, just as he was gaining consciousness.

"I'm sorry, Alpha," he'd said the minute his eyes fluttered open. He was apologizing for not guarding my Howl, for letting her get hurt.

"We'll all do better in the future with her," I'd said, feeling ashamed. Just like my father, I'd allowed my Howl to be put in danger and hurt.

"I know you're there, watching me," Neera said quietly from the shore, drawing my attention and thoughts to the present, to her.

"I am, little Howl. I want to be near you, but I wasn't going to interrupt."

She shrugged. "You can come sit."

I sat as close as I could to her, both my wolf and I needing her near us. For a while we just sat without words, Neera watching the water and me watching Neera.

"I hate that they had to be sacrificed," she whispered after a while.

I shook my head at her words. "They offered themselves as sacrifices, Neera. There's a big difference. You've never been in a war, and I hope to the Forces you never will be, but both Blaisall and Lindsay Morgan have, so they knew the gesture that you don't."

"What gesture?" She finally looked over at me, her eyes curious.

"When an Alpha is preparing his wolves for battle, he gives them a pre-victory speech to help ramp them up for success. At the end of his speech, all of his warriors lift their heads up, either as wolf or human, exposing their necks to the Alpha. It's not only a gesture of submission to the Alpha, but a gesture meaning take my life, which I offer to you, for this pack," I explained. "Blaisall and Lindsay Morgan's wolves both did that. Immediately and without hesitation. They knew, Neera. They knew what needed to happen to stop the magicks. They'd been living with them, and they both knew first-hand the evil they were capable of."

"Ifrita said Lindsay Morgan had just met her Destined One when she found them together in the woods. And Lindsay allowed him to be killed so she could keep her life."

"Unforgiveable," Night said, his voice harsh. "You fight for your Destined One or die together. She probably was easier for Ifrita to repress because the pain of being separated from her Destined One was destroying her just as much as Ifrita was. Lindsay Morgan would not have lasted long even if we had found a way to save her and kill the magick. She had three years of guilt and pain."

My Howl's little head was bowed still, and my wolf and I did not like her sad thoughts. I ran my hand over her hair, hoping to soothe her.

"She died nobly, little Howl. There is no greater honor for a wolf in battle, and make no mistake -- that was a war for our lives and for the pack's lives and for all packs' lives. It was her choice, and although she didn't make the right choice with her Destined One, Lindsay Morgan made the right choice in the end."

"And Blaisall?"

"You saw her. She also offered her neck. Four hundred years of living with the agony of being a rejected mate and the pain of having an evil magick share her body...she was ready to go to the Forces after centuries of suffering. She wanted to be at peace, Neera."

My Howl was silent as she thought about all that I'd told her.

When she turned her head to look at me, tears were swimming in her eyes. "And what about you? Hearing about...about your parents." She practically choked on the last words.

"I knew how my parents died, Neera. I knew it was horrible."

"But to hear it..."

"And to know I was with my parents' killer for three years. Regardless that I was enchanted or spelled or whatever the fuck she did to me, it still burns me inside, makes me feel sick, makes me want to kill her all over again, thousands of time, each time more painful than the last. And to know how I hurt you? Each time I think about it, I feel like I'm being stabbed in the heart. I really am sorry, Neera."

She sighed. "I know I should say I forgive you, but that feels wrong because there's really nothing to forgive in that sense. It wasn't you doing any of that. It was her."

"There might have been one or two things, though, that were me."

"The trunk was all you," Neera said sourly.

"Done for your safety, based on my dreams. All I could think about was keeping you safe, and yet I still failed in that."

"You saved me, saved all of us, in the end. I don't think you failed at all."

"You were hurt," I said softly, looking at her fading bruises. "That's unacceptable."

"But not killed," she reminded me. "You saved us all from two very powerful magicks."

Sensing she needed a change of subject, I slid a long rectangular box out of my shirt pocket and handed it to Neera. "I promised you I'd buy you something nice for your birthday gift."

She shot me a look.

"Open it," I prodded her. "I don't wrap gifts, but I promise it is one."

She lifted the lid off the box and drew out the long silver chain that held a silver locket with an inscribed N on the front in curly script. She opened it and pressed her lips together. I'd had one of the older artists in the pack who had known her parents paint tiny portraits of her mother and her father, one for each side of the locket.

"I hardly have any pictures of my parents," she said, unable to tear her eyes away from the pictures. "Thank you. Thank you."

"You're welcome, little Howl."

I watched her stare at the portraits for a few more minutes before she closed the locket and slipped the necklace over her head.

"Also wanted to catch you up with some decisions I've made. The prison house, as you called it, and my old house are being burned down today," I said. "Everything in them will be turned to ash and then the cement pads will be bulldozed so nothing of either house remains. I'm building a new house for us on Crescent Lake, but I want you to choose the plans for the house you want and see if you like the lot I'm thinking of."

She nodded, whether in approval of my plan to burn down the houses or agreeing to select the house plans I couldn't tell.

"I know I've pushed you and ruined our Taking of the Blood, but I'm not pushing any more, Neera, I promise. You're my Howl, and even though my instinct is to move fast with you, I can take it slow. It's going to take about five months for our house to be built, and we're going to use that time to get to know each other without the pressure of needing to save the wolf world on our shoulders."

At that, my wolf went wild, unhappy with that decision and possibly down right pissed off.

What? Take it slow? Noooooooo! Just get her on all fours and she'll love you when you fuck --

She gave a half smile. "You're telling me you're going to spend the next few months...wooing me?"

"Yes. I won't push for anything physical. We'll just use this time to get to know one another and the timeline for how and when we move forward is in your hands since I took so much out of your hands -- regardless of my reasons. It'll give you time to let certain memories fade a bit so they aren't so fresh and raw."

What the hell kind of bullshit idea is this?! Woo her with your dick!

Yep. He was definitely pissed off.

"If you want, you can go back to your apartment until our house is ready. You'll still have a guard, but you don't have to stay with me."

No! No! No! Our Howl should be with us!

"OK," she said slowly. "I have a lot to think about and sort through in my mind, so I appreciate having a little time."

What does she need to think about?

Looking at Neera's face, I felt for my overwhelmed little Howl. Even though it went against every instinct I had, she needed a little space, and I could give her that now that we had Taken the Blood and the threat from the magicks was gone. I didn't have my dreams pressing on me so I could relax a little.

Taking her hand in mine, I let her absorb some of my Alpha energy that every member of the pack needed, but she especially needed right now.

"The way you behaved yesterday, Neera -- I know it was terrifying, but you made me so damn proud. Our pack has been without a Howl for far too long. You're everything we need and more, and not a day will go by that I don't thank the Forces for sending you to me, to our pack."

She didn't say anything, but she did squeeze my hand.

And for now, that was enough.

Chapter 17: Alpha

An Alpha set on wooing his Howl is a man who doesn't know exactly what the hell to do with himself. An Alpha had never before had to woo his Howl -- basic biological urges took care of that for him and everything fell neatly into place as the two came together, tearing off clothes to get at one another in a frantic frenzy, canines descending a bit, eyes glowing, little growls coming out instead of words at times.

Because Night had given his word to me that we'd take it slow, he was having to fight both his nature and his wolf -- and he was doing it to give me time. To settle. To process all of the craziness that had taken place since my birthday. For an Alpha, that was a huge concession.

I know I've pushed you and ruined our Taking of the Blood, but I'm not pushing any more, Neera, I promise. You're my Howl, and even though my instinct is to move fast with you, I can take it slow.

My instinct made me want to move faster, too, but I fought it and made sure we were moving slowly. Of course I knew where we'd end up. That was given, a foregone conclusion that was absolutely inevitable, but I wasn't taking the direct path there. The human part of me liked the idea of being pursued and dated, building a relationship that was based on feelings and not instinctual urges.

It's going to take about five months for our house to be built, and we're going to use that time to get to know each other without the pressure of needing to save the wolf world on our shoulders.

We may not have had the pressure of saving the wolf world on our shoulders, but we sure as hell had the pressure of hormones -- out of control, raging, intense, unrelenting -- on our shoulders. Every time I was near him, my wolf sat up, right along with my human hormones and reached out for him. And the man knew it, because his canines would descend and he'd fill his lungs with me, then turn and stalk away a few yards, muttering to himself. Although maybe he was fighting his wolf, because I'd heard him snap, I'm not humping her damn leg, so just shut the fuck up about that! one time in utter frustration.

But for an Alpha who didn't know exactly how to woo his Howl, he was making a surprisingly good effort -- he was funny, he was a little goofy, he was eager to please and he was charming as hell. But underneath all of it was a sweetness that couldn't be denied. He was like a...wolf pup, bouncing energy, happy to be around me, wanting my attention and lapping up any notice I gave him.

With every other pack member, he was Alpha -- decisive, controlling, firm, caring, rock-steady. Strong as hell. I was getting another side of him that no other pack member ever had, not even Lindsay Morgan when Ifrita was controlling her. For three years, despite being enchanted to believe he was in love with Lindsay Morgan, Night had never behaved toward her the way he was acting with me.

I thought back to the day after we had killed the magicks, when we honored the wolves who had offered their necks so Raevyn and Ifrita could be destroyed. We all gathered around the bonfire as Night addressed all of us.

"We honor Blaisall and Lindsay Morgan today, for without their obedience to a decree, without their willingness to lift up their heads and show their throats, our pack would no longer be. We send them, with our thanks, on their journey back home."

Solemnly, we all watched as their wolves' bodies turned to ash so they would become part of the earth again, and their spirits would ride to the Forces on the flames that leapt up into the sky. I searched Night's face for any signs of distress for Lindsay Morgan's death, I even reached out through our bond, but there was nothing except gratitude that she and Blaisall had bared their necks.

He sought me out after he touched hands with all of the pack members. The rumors had been flying about exactly what had gone down the previous day, and everyone needed reassurance through the Alpha's touch to calm and help settle them down.

I lingered beside him as the last of the wolves left the funeral pyre, and he pressed his hand to the back of my head, smoothing my hair.

"I feel better with them burned and the houses they were in burned," Night said suddenly. "I wanted to make sure no lingering magic survived, if that was even a remote possibility."

"That makes sense," I agreed, "since we don't know exactly what we were dealing with or what they were capable of."

"They were capable of great destruction," he said with sadness, then he turned to me. "I don't want you thinking I feel anything for her. I felt you searching through the bond, and you couldn't find anything because there's nothing there. Magic made me say I had feelings for her, but it was never anything real."

"I know," I said. "I just wanted to make sure. Three years..."

"You never need to worry, little Howl. My affections are focused on you and only you."

I'd played with the locket he'd given me the day before. "I know, Alpha," I said using the name I hadn't used for him respectfully since my ill-fated birthday.

"Don't," he said sharply, his body suddenly going rigid.

"Don't what?"

"Don't call me Alpha like that. From pack members, it's a title of respect, of acknowledging my authority. But from you, Neera, it's a verbal signal that I'm your Alpha and you're my Howl...and you're offering me your submission so I can fucking dominate you."

"Oh-kay," I said, making a mental note not to use that term.

Yet.

"I'm going to do my damnedest to take it slow with you, Neera. You deserve that after what you went through. But when I tell you that it's going to take a lot of control, trust me on that. My wolf is driving me hard to take you, and I'm right there with him, but my human side still has control. I need you not to test that."

So I was careful not to push him, partly because I had wanted to see what taking it slow was like. If it was even something wolves were capable of. We never really got the chance to fall in love -- you found your Destined One and were drawn together and the feelings were intense -- and then those feelings just naturally became love? Or were those feelings called love because the physical aspect of the relationship was so overwhelmingly powerful? I'd wondered that as I'd watched Destined Ones together. Would they be together if they hadn't been brought together by the Forces? Would they have ever found each other otherwise?

Wanting to find out the answers to those questions helped me to take it slow -- that and pushing back my wolf when she wanted to come out and play. I knew she hated waiting -- when Night had decreed the shift, she was already in motion, heading to bite him right away. Wolves were pure instinct and urge...it was our human sides that had to develop and grow feelings.

I let Night woo me, as he called it. I think the whole pack was watching, amused, baffled, entertained. Every time he saw me, he'd stop what he was doing and head over to me. When I went to the Den for my meals, he was always there, on the lookout for me.

"Hi, Neera," he'd say all happy-eyed and smiling. Smiling! As Alpha, he was serious, somewhat stern-faced, but his face was practically shining with joy when he came near me. If he'd been shifted, his tail would have been going a mile a minute. "I saved you a seat at my table. Do you and your friends want to sit with us?"

Us was Aymeric and Néron. I looked at Echo and Owena and they shrugged, so we went over to join them, Night walking right beside me. Smiling.

"Here, you can sit right next to me," Night said as he pulled out a chair for me.

"Thanks," I smiled back at him, trying not to laugh at his eagerness as my friends found chairs for themselves.

"Hey, Meri," Echo said. "Nice to see you using utensils. Didn't know you had that skill."

Aymeric slammed down his fork and knife and pointed a finger at Echo. "Watch your mouth, little wolf."

"Why?" she shot back. "Was utensils too big of a word for you to understand?"

"So," I interrupted, trying to prevent a murder. Whose I wasn't sure, but I strongly suspected Aymeric was almost coming out of his skin. Echo seemed to rub him the wrong way. "Anyone binge watch any good shows lately?"

"No, but if you want, we could watch TV tonight," Night offered, leaning close. I turned suddenly, and I swear -- no kidding -- he'd been about to lick my face. What the fuck?

"Sure, we can do that," I agreed. He backed away a bit, still smiling, eyes shining.

Night had to stay to touch hands with the pack members after we finished dinner, and Owena was laughing at him on our way out the door. My ever-present guard followed closely behind.

"You're going to make Alpha lose his mind," she said. "He's never going to make it until your house is built."

"He'll be fine. He's just like a...like a happy little boy around me."

"He's like a happy little boy when you look at him," Echo said. "But when you aren't looking -- hoo, boy. He's almost savage the way he watches you."

"Like he's about to take you to the ground and put you on all fours," Owena added.

"He promised to give me time."

"Yeah," Owena said. "Night promised. That doesn't mean his wolf's on board with the plan."

So, here we were, four months after we honored Blaisall and Lindsay Morgan, about a month before our house was ready, and Night was getting ready to leave my apartment after spending the evening with me, as he always did. I knew that the minute he left, he'd shift and run for half the night because he had some serious energy he needed to expend. Every time I saw him lately, his wolf was making himself known and Night was having to back him down more and more frequently. Keeping his word was requiring tremendous restraint, especially on Night's part, but his promise to me was important to him.

And our months together had been...beautiful. Illuminating. I discovered there was so much more to Night than I ever suspected, than he ever showed to his pack. He was no longer just Alpha to me; he was a man with great depth and thoughtfulness and consideration. Even sweetness, and that aspect, I knew, was solely for me. No one else would ever get that like I did. As I was falling in love with him, I hoped he was discovering things about me that he liked just as well, and that he was falling for me, too.

Tonight, as he stood up from my couch, his wolf was right there and Night was looking a wee bit feral. The veins in his neck were straining, and his muscles were flexing and rippling as he fought his wolf for supremacy.

"I can't even kiss you goodnight right now," he said, and his voice was harsh and guttural. "Go open the door so I can just run out of here and then close it behind me fast."

Nodding, I hurried toward the door and had just barely opened it when a large hand slammed it shut from above my head. I heard a low, throaty growl right behind me and Night's massive body was pressed tight against me.

At that moment, I realized my mistake: I'd turned my back on a predator who was teetering on the edge of self control.

And who was now losing the fight after all these months of denying that very basic biological urge inherent in our natures. I stilled, hardly daring to breathe, knowing any move on my part could trigger Night into losing the battle.

He ran his nose alongside my neck, his breathing harsh and ragged so close to my ear.

"Your scent is in my very skin," he rasped. "I can smell your need for me, and I want to lap at that need before I bury my cock in you, Neera."

Then he drew his tongue down my neck and bit into that irresistible place where my neck met my shoulder. His teeth gripped my skin and held on for a minute. Then he growled again and let go, his tongue lapping at the small wound.

"Tell me to go," he ordered me. "I can. I can."

"Actually," I said, turning in his arms, "I think I'd like you to stay."

He slammed me back against the door, and lowered his face right to mine, his hand on my throat, holding me in place. Our eyes were locked on each other, intense.

I paused a moment before adding breathlessly, "Alpha."

Chapter 18: Good Girl

I tried. I fucking tried. For months, I'd beaten back my wolf, much to his disgust and displeasure. As the weeks wore on, he became bolder, and then two months in, he began fighting me for dominance, trying to force my hand, to finally claim my Howl the way an Alpha should.

Pups, pups, pups.

He'd chant that at me, knowing it was my weakness, knowing as Alpha, the need to breed my Howl was overwhelming and the desire to see her filled with my pups was almost as necessary as the air I needed to breathe. As Alpha, I settled the pack members with my touch, but now that I had found my Howl and Taken her Blood, nothing would settle me until I had given her my child.

"Be prepared," my father had warned me not long before I turned twenty-one. "It's a compulsion like no other. You think you're prepared for your Howl; you think you understand how you'll feel, but you do not. Your Howl will become your obsession and breeding her your overriding objective in life until you succeed."

He'd been right. But I felt even more strongly that Neera needed time, and I gave us the five months until our new house would be completed to move ahead. My little Howl, after what she'd seen and heard and experienced, definitely needed some time.

Since no one in the pack had ever dated a Destined One before, I had no one to ask for advice, so I Googled romantic shit to do for your girl and went from there. We did picnics by a stream, rowing boats on one of the Aibek lakes, early morning hikes to watch the sunrise, sitting side-by-side on a bench by a lake to watch the sunset, dinner out at restaurants, and evenings in together. Watching Neera enjoy our times together settled me to some extent, but the fucking wolf was always in my ear.

Push her down on the blanket. Shove your sandwich in her basket and show her a real picnic.

Rock the boat. Rock it!

Watch the sunrise over her back. Do it!

Every day, I made sure to bring her a little something to show her I'd listened to her the day before.

Some days, it was chocolate-covered strawberries.

Some days, it was a new nail polish color she'd mentioned.

Other days, it was fresh blueberries and wildflowers.

On some other days, I would sit and brush that gorgeous hair of hers for a long, long time, then put aside the brush and lift the strands in my hands and let them fall around her shoulders.

Wrap it in your fist and show her why long hair can be fun. Use the brush on her ass --

But all those weeks and months, Neera and I talked, most of all. By tacit agreement, we didn't reach through the bond for the other's thoughts and feelings so we had to communicate in a way no other Alpha and Howl ever had before. For once, our human natures were building a relationship first, not after we came together.

I liked best those evenings with her on her couch, where we held hands or she cuddled into me and I pulled her onto my lap so I could just breathe her in, each inhale soothing a bit of the pain we had gone through to get to this moment.

When I couldn't take the closeness anymore without threatening to break the promise I made her, I'd kiss her good night and reluctantly leave her place. Nodding to the guard outside her door, I'd shift the minute she closed and locked the door behind me and run until I was so exhausted, I dragged my tail back to the Den where I kept a room. Then I might get a few hours of sleep until my wolf woke me and we'd agree it'd been too many hours since we'd last seen our Howl.

It was a special time that was both frustrating and eye-opening. Each day I spent with my little Howl, each word from her mouth that I treasured like gold, each fleeting touch from her fingertips built and built in my heart until I knew that I not only desired her as my Destined One -- my Howl -- but I loved her as a woman and respected her as a partner who would stand beside me for life.

So fuck her already!

My wolf was rapidly losing patience with me, so much so that I found myself currently pressing Neera against her apartment door, my hand wrapped around her throat looking right into her eyes.

I knew she saw my wolf peeking out.

And from the way her eyes widened, she liked it.

Then she uttered the one word that would push us past the point of no return.

"Alpha."

One word. One desperate word.

It hung in the air between us, breathless, needy and hungry, which meant she was breathless and needy and hungry.

And even more, it was submissive. My little Howl wanted me to dominate her, to make her submit to me, and there was no fucking way I could ignore that unspoken plea.

I felt her pulse racing under my fingertips and I wanted to replace my fingers with my teeth and force her to the ground and rip her pants off and shove my throbbing, aching cock into her --

I drew in a sharp breath. This was going to be over before it barely started if I didn't get my fucking wolf under control.

I tightened my grip on her neck just enough to make her eyes widen, then I leaned in close, pressing my lips to her ear.

"Are you going to be my good girl, little Howl? Are you going to let me do whatever I want to you?"

I could feel her swallow against my hand as she nodded.

"Words, Neera. Tell me in words. Tell me."

"I'm going to be your good girl...Alpha."

Titanium was harder than steel, and even then I was pretty fucking sure my dick was harder than that at this point. I had to make our first time together special, memorable, not some animalistic mating that would end with me throwing her to the ground on all fours and pounding into her until my seed was pouring into her. We'd get there, that was unavoidable, but I wanted to start out slower tonight.

Shit. I needed my motherfucking head examined.

Stepping back from Neera, I picked her up by the waist and spun her around so she was still facing me, but my back was now to the door.

"Go to your room, baby. I'm holding on by a thread here, so don't turn your back to me or this won't be what I'm trying so hard to give you."

Neera held my eyes and backed up one step.

Then two.

And then she fucking turned her back on me and ran.

Game. Over.

In one leap, I was on her, grabbing her around the waist, taking her to the ground, but turning so I absorbed the fall. Quickly flipping her over so she was on her back, I saw those beautiful, plush lips smiling coyly at me.

She had me right where she wanted me -- over her -- and I had her right where I wanted her -- under me.

Grabbing her hands, I slammed them down on the floor above her head, one hand holding both her wrists together. My mouth was on hers before she could say a word, tongues tangling, teeth nipping and biting, as I tore at our clothes with my free hand, claws out, until we were both naked.

When a starving man is offered a feast, he doesn't even know where to start. As I looked down at Neera's tits, her hips and thighs and finally at that juicy cunt that was already dripping with need for me -- for her Alpha -- I was ready to descend on her like a fucking animal.

Slow down.

I palmed her breast with one hand, thumbing her nipple while my mouth worked its way down her neck, biting hard when she tried to move her hands from my grip.

"Leave them there," I warned her, barely recognizing the harsh and primal voice as my own.

She did as told, and to reward her, I took her nipple into my mouth, tugging on it with my teeth then nipping just hard enough to make her back arch off the floor as she whimpered.

Submitting.

I moved my mouth from one breast to the other, biting, soothing, licking, tugging her little nipples on repeat until she was mindless, writhing under me, her pussy instinctively searching for my cock.

Not yet.

Continuing to torment her tits with my mouth, I covered her pussy with my hand, drenching my palm with her juices.

Lifting my head, I locked my eyes on hers, brought my hand to my mouth and inhaled while she watched me lick my hand.

"Your scent intoxicates me," I said, "And your taste makes your Alpha hungry."

I kissed my way down her belly to her mound, and pressed a kiss to her clit, just to hear her gasp and feel her arch, wanting my mouth on her.

I bit her thigh sharply. "Wait."

That just seemed to inflame her more and she began to plead with me. "Please," my Howl begged, her voice breathless. I loved the need and desire that indicated and wanted to pull more of that sound from her.

So I kissed that soaked cunt, wanting to just bury my face in her wetness, drown myself in her addictive scent, but I held myself back and began lapping lightly at her slit, enough so she noticed but not enough to do anything but tease. I kept at it until she began whimpering, and I had to hold her hips down so she couldn't force my tongue deeper.

When I felt her hands in my hair, I again bit Neera on her thigh, and she jumped.

"Keep your hands above your head," I ordered her. She hesitated, and I nipped at her thigh again. "Now, little Howl, or I stop."

That was a fucking lie -- I couldn't stop now if my life depended on it, but the threat seemed to work, and I looked up Neera's body to see her hands stretched above her head, back arched, tits up, nipples still glistening from my mouth's ministrations.

I spread her legs apart and my mouth began working that hot pussy, trying to lick every bit of desire from her. My thumbs moved her lips apart as I licked her deeper and deeper, and then I moved slightly to suck on her clit as I curled one finger inside of her until she began moaning my name.

Now.

I ripped my mouth away from my frantic Howl and in one move flipped her over so she was on all fours. I knelt behind her, using one hand to press the head of my cock at the entrance of her pussy. With the other hand, I gripped the back of her neck, forcing her head down to the carpet, which presented her pussy to me in a way that made me want to howl.

"Tell me who you belong to," I commanded her in a voice more wolf than human.

"To you," she responded immediately. "To my Alpha." So breathless.

"Good girl," I said and then immediately rewarded her by slamming my cock into her fully, relishing Neera's gasp of pleasure and pain.

Removing my hand from her neck, I grasped her hips in my hands and began pounding into her delicious cunt that I'd denied myself for so long. Every thrust, I seated myself into her fully, then withdrew until just the tip of my cock was inside her...just to slam back into her.

Over and over, until she was almost sobbing, begging me to make her come, her hands grasping at the floor. Grabbing a handful of her hair, I pulled back until she was up on her knees, and I continued fucking her, one hand holding her breast to hold her in place and the other moving to stroke her clit, slicking it with her wetness as I continued fucking into her.

Her pussy gripped my dick like a fucking vice and when I felt my balls tighten, felt that tingling at the base of my spine, I knew I was close.

"Come for me, Neera," I whispered in her ear.

And my good girl fucking exploded on my say-so with a sharp cry, shuddering and sobbing my name, held tight in my arms.

Unable to resist my Howl's pleasure rippling around my cock, I came and came hard, pouring my seed into her, filling her up until our combined pleasure was dripping onto my balls, her thighs.

I pressed my mouth to her neck as we waited for our breathing to even out, and I never wanted to let her go.

But I knew I had one thing left to do to wipe any lingering memories from her mind.

I withdrew my cock from her, and turned her to face me, still on our knees.

"Lick me clean," I said and she froze.

I cupped her jaw and looked into her eyes.

"Yes," I told her softly but firmly. "This is between us. Night and Neera and nobody else. I won't have that lingering to torment you, little Howl. I won't stand for something like that between us. I want you to own this, own every part of me. I want you to take it back and make it yours."

I felt her search the bond.

I pressed a kiss to her lips. "You already own my heart, little Howl. Now I want you to take it all and claim it as your own."

And fuck me running, she lowered her mouth to my cock and took back her power.

Chapter 19: What Is His Name?

I'd known for a long time the basic truth that life was constantly chang-ing.

It changed the day my parents were killed in the Aibek-Lunaire pack war, and I became an orphan along with many other wolves.

It changed the day I woke up and discovered I was the Alpha's Howl, and my excitement was off the charts with the thought of belonging to someone again, and not just the pack as a whole.

It changed again when Night rejected me, and I suffered the pain of being cast aside by my Destined One.

It changed again after he Took my Blood, and I hated him for biting me without my consent.

It changed yet again after I bit him, and we bonded, connected, and in doing so, helped save the pack from two evil magicks.

And it changed last night, when Night finally tackled me to the floor and fucked me for hours.

The last time, we'd finally made it to my bed, and when we'd both come so hard we could barely do more than breathe, Night eventually summoned the energy to roll to his back, with me on top, his cock connecting us. Alphas, I'd discovered, could stay hard for hours, even after they'd come.

"Go to sleep, little Howl," he ordered me gruffly. As directed, I settled more comfortably on top of him, taking his hard cock even deeper inside of me, and laid my head on his chest. His arms went around me, pressing me closer to his heart.

My last thought before I fell asleep was that I loved being connected to this man both physically and emotionally. The feeling of being so intimately joined with him was reassuring, both to me and my wolf. For the first time in years, we had a family again; we were no longer alone in the pack.

When I woke up, his arms were still around me, and never in my life had I felt safer or so well loved. That Night loved me I had no doubt; I'd searched our bond at one point, while I was on my back, and Night was thrusting slowly, deliciously into me, looking down to see where we were joined, when his head suddenly came up and he looked into my eyes.

"More than anything," he'd said simply in response to my unvoiced question. "You don't even have to search our bond. If you ever wonder, just look in my eyes. They hold everything I feel for you in them and they always will."

This morning, he came alert the moment I moved and smiled lazily at me.

"Good morning, little Howl." He popped a kiss on the tip of my nose. "I liked you falling asleep with my cock in you. I'm looking forward to that every night after I fill you with my seed."

I smiled at him. "You're going to fill me just at night?"

His smile became an arrogant grin. "I'll fill you with my seed whenever I want, Neera. As an Alpha, I'm very single minded in my dedication and determination to fill my Howl with my pups."

"Well, at the rate you're going, it won't take long." And I couldn't wait. If Night was driven to breed me, I was just as instinctually driven to be bred, to grow ripe with my Alpha's child.

He smiled at that and rolled me to my back, his ginormous hand splayed over my belly.

"Someday soon, I'm going to feel the future Aibek Alpha moving around in you. Then his brothers and sisters will follow until we have so many you're going to threaten to cut off my balls," he teased me.

"As long as you keep adding on to the house, I don't care how many we have."

That made Night smile huge, and he hugged me to him. "We'll see who cries uncle first, little Howl."

When we were getting ready to head to the Den for breakfast, Night turned to me. "If I let you go find a wedding dress today, do you promise it won't take you three weeks to find it?" Hmmm, apparently someone was still a bit salty that I'd run away from him for three weeks.

"Oh, are we getting married?" I asked him archly. "I wasn't aware I'd been asked."

Night grunted. "And you won't be. You're mine, little Howl. We're getting married tonight, so go out with your girls and get a dress today." He paused a minute and looked me up and down. "Or wear what you have on now."

For the record, I was naked.

"Tonight?!" I screeched. "I can't find a dress that fast --"

"Makes no difference to me. Dress or not, we're getting married tonight, when the moon rises. Now, do what I say and I'll reward my good girl later." Then, with one hand grabbing my hair, he pressed a hard kiss to my lips and walked out the door, leaving his Howl spluttering behind him.

And, not going to lie, kind of looking forward to later.

Welp, no breakfast at the Den for me. Or for Owena and Echo. I sent them an SOS NEED DRESSES FOR TONIGHT FOR ALL OF US text and within fifteen minutes, we were on our way. Of course, my trusty guard drove us in the huge SUV Night insisted I take if I went anywhere, and two hours into our excursion, I could practically hear him grinding his molars as we rushed from store to store.

Echo found her dress first, a light baby blue color that worked well with her blonde hair. Then I found a simple but elegant cream-colored dress that had a tightly fitted bodice and flared out into a fluffy skirt. Owena finally found hers in the last store we went to, and the dark pink sheath set off her figure beautifully.

On the way back, Echo was furiously texting on her phone. "What's going on?" I asked her.

"Listen, just because Alpha said you're getting married tonight with no notice doesn't mean we can't have a beautiful wedding for you. So I told Aymeric to rally every single member of the pack or I'd kick his ass by using a lot of multi-syllable words. I was just checking in to get an update on the to-do list I sent him-- I wasn't even sure if he even knew how to read -- and there's currently a huge cake being decorated, tons and tons of food being made, decorations being put up, twinkle lights being hung, a little arch for you and Night to stand under being built and decorated, chairs being put out for the pack and flowers being arranged. When we get back, hair and makeup are waiting for you. The end."

Owena and I just stared at her. She stared back. "What? You think I would stand for some lame-ass wedding for one of my besties? Fuck that noise. Besides, it's fun making Aymeric run around like my little bitch."

"Well, she has a point," Owena said, looking from Echo to me. Then her eyes brightened. "Oh, oh, oh! Tell him that Neera has her heart set on Night's two best men also holding bouquets of flowers to match ours. And remind him that a request from the Howl is just as compelling as a request from Alpha."

Echo's eyes gleamed evilly and she shot off a text to the big bad Alpha's Teeth. She nibbled on her lower lip as she waited for his reply and suddenly looked up at us with triumph.

"He said OK, which means he will honor the Howl's wishes. Yes!" Fist pumps and high fives all around.

"Do you think we could get away with saying that Neera wants Aymeric and Néron in tutus and tiaras?" Owena always did like to push the boundaries.

"No!" I protested, laughing. "Having them holding flowers is bad enough."

"Yeah, we want to keep this wedding classy as fuck," Echo said, seriously, then wondered why Owena and I started laughing at her.

Two seconds after we cleared the gate allowing us back onto pack lands, Night texted me.

Glad that didn't take three weeks.

The man thought he was hilarious. Before I could snark back, he sent another text.

Naked would have been fine.

That made me laugh.

Then came the best text of all.

Néron and Aymeric need flowers?

I let the girls see that text, which set us all off, so much so that it was hard for me to type out an answer.

It's really important to me that they hold bouquets during the wedding.

Let's see what he did with that.

Then it will happen. Anything to please my Howl.

"That has unlimited possibilities," Owena mused thoughtfully.

They'll carry flowers, but your ass will pay for it later tonight. Don't think I don't know what you're doing, little Howl.

That text I didn't share with my friends. But my wolf and I both couldn't wait for tonight.

While my hair was being whipped into shape and my makeup was being expertly applied so I didn't look like a clown, Echo and Owena were running around to make sure everything was on schedule and looking perfect. The funny thing to me was that they were more into the details of the wedding than I was. I would have been happy if Night and I had recited our vows to each other by ourselves, under the moon.

Hours later, the three of us were dressed and ready to go, and the girls handed me the traditional blood-red rose bouquet that wolf brides traditionally carried.

Echo and Owena had pretty large bouquets with trailing ribbons.

"Bigger and fussier than I'd normally have chosen," Echo said indicating her flowers, "but the guys are carrying the same exact ones, so...they can't be missed."

A knock on the door from the guard told us it was time.

"OK, we got this," Owena said, softly.

It was our traditional battle cry, so to speak, when we were embarking on something new. We'd said it when we started high school. We'd said it when we graduated. We'd said it when we'd begun our jobs. We'd said it when we parted ways the night before my twenty-first birthday.

And now, I was the first one to be marrying my Destined One. Echo would be next, her birthday being just a week away. Provided her Destined One was in the pack, we could be right back here in no time.

"We got this," Echo agreed. They both looked at me.

"We got this," I said, and my eyes started filling with tears.

"Don't you dare cry," Owena threatened me with a finger pointed at my nose. "I'll fuck you up if you ruin all that hard work that was done on your face."

So it was that I walked down the aisle, laughing. Admittedly, seeing Néron and Aymeric standing proud and tall beside Night, holding their pretty pink and white bouquets, might also have added to that.

The actual wedding ceremony didn't take long. Night, who, as Alpha, always married couples, now found himself in the position of marrying us, and we said the age old words that had joined two Destined Ones forever. But at the end, he added something new, as he addressed our pack.

"The Forces, in their wisdom, send each of us the perfect partner. I have never disagreed with their pairings, but I have to say, in giving me Neera

Karis, they have outdone themselves. My Howl is brave and kind and strong, and she complements me in every way. It will be my honor to love her for the rest of my days."

He kissed my hand, tipped back his head and howled his appreciation to the Forces. Every member of the pack joined in the howl, lifting their faces to the moon, letting our wolves share in the celebration in this small but important way.

Later that evening, when Night and I were sharing our first dance, I looked around at the eyes of our pack members watching us intently, knowing they were soothed by this, knowing this image would replace the memory of their Alpha's rejection of me.

"The memory will fade, with time," Night said, low in my ear. "I only hope you can someday forget."

"I will because I know it wasn't really you," I said.

"And maybe because you will be too busy with our son in nine months," he said. "Our pup is already growing in you, Neera."

I smiled at him, feeling my happiness about to bubble over at the thought. "And how do you know this so fast?"

"I know because the Forces sent me an Alpha Dream last night. They do that to give me the name of the next Alpha."

"And what is his name?"

Night smiled at me. "He will be called Darius, and he will be the first of many, little Howl."

Yep, life would continue to change, and that sounded pretty perfect to me.

Epilogue: A Simple Statement Of Truth

F ive years later...

The years since I married my little Howl have seemed like but a moment in time. I may be Alpha of the Aibek pack, but she is the ruler of me. Everything I do is with the aim of making her happy, and although I don't always succeed completely because I'm a man and I can be dense, it's my goal everyday to make her smile, make her laugh, make her thankful the Forces joined us together.

And to give her good dick every day, most important of all!

He's still a horny little fucker, my wolf.

My eyes are always on my Howl whenever I'm in the same room with her, and I try to make that as often as possible, unless I have pack business to attend to. Neera right now is making her way toward me and our three children are beside her, with their guards following them. It is like watching your very heart walk toward you. Darius, at a little over four, refuses to hold Neera's hand in the Den, which breaks my wife's heart, but outwardly she just rolls her eyes and blames me.

"He acts just like you, Night," she says, exasperated with his pint-sized Alpha attitude. "In every way possible -- he's arrogant, independent, ready to fight, and he struts around like the future Alpha he is."

I shrug, knowing she's right, trying not to let her see just how proud I am of our son, of his aggressiveness, of his need to dominate. He'll need those qualities to rule the Aibek pack someday. But I also know that he's still very much a little boy; Darius snuggles on what little lap Neera has whenever possible, his ear against her heart, letting the sound soothe him. His mother's heartbeat calms all that confusing need for dominance and control inside of him so I've asked Neera to be especially watchful for him wanting his heartbeat time. All wolf pups find it soothing, but future Alphas find it especially so.

Alphas, even from a very young age, are cocky, fearless, and much, much more aggressive than other boys their age, preparing for their future place in the pack. While most wolves shift at around age five, future Alphas shift even earlier -- Darius shifted for the first time right after his third birthday, and fortunately I was there because he took off after our cat. Neera would have a fit if her gray tabby, Sleek, became our son's first kill.

At that young age, the wolf and the human haven't learned to work together yet and the wolf is a primal creature going on instinct alone with no human to hold him back. So that day, I picked up the tiny little wolf by the scruff of his neck, and I fucking Alpha decreed his little ass to never hurt the cat. The little bastard still tried to nip me on the nose with a snap of those tiny jaws, but my wolf answered that unwise little challenge with a bone-chilling growl that made my son's wolf whine. My wolf might love our pups, but he knew when a lesson needed to be learned.

Darius occasionally forgets his mother's place in our immediate family pack, and when he does, I take him out to the woods where we shift and I remind him who is Alpha with a lot of snarling, growling and snapping my teeth at him, accompanied by the occasional nip on his flank or swipe of my paw. It's a language his wolf understands as I teach him about hierarchy. His mother takes precedence over everyone but me and, as such, she will be respected; Darius will settle for a time after a lesson in the woods...until his wolf pushes forward again and the lesson will be repeated. And it will continue to be repeated until he and his wolf figure things out between them and they both learn control and pecking order.

Neera probably suspects what really goes on when I suggest a walk in the woods with my son so we can talk, but she has never asked and I'll keep that from her so she doesn't have to worry about Darius.

She has enough to worry about with all three children and the baby who's almost here. Our fourth child in five years is starting to settle that need I feel to breed Neera, but she hasn't said a word about wanting to be done, and I'm happy to keep her filled with my pups. My wolf fucking struts around still chanting pups pups pups so I know there are more in our future. I already have an architect working on plans for an addition to our house, and even though she hasn't had this baby yet, Neera's already talking about our next.

My Howl's convinced our fifth child will be a girl, which she needs to balance out the testosterone in our house. The other three boys may not be Alphas like Darius, but they come from the Alpha line, so they are already more rough and tumble than most other wolf pups their age -- just not to the extent that Darius is. As the oldest, he's their leader and closest friend, and I encourage their dependency on one another because that family bond is critical.

Néron remains my closest friend, with Aymeric a close second, and I would have Darius surrounded by strong wolves he can depend on. So far, my two other boys, Taggart and Forje, show every sign of being sub-alphas, and I suspect that Forje will become the Alpha's Teeth. He's going to be a big boy, almost as big as Darius, and he's only three but is willing to take on Darius. Watching them fight in the yard, I observe the way they take each other down, and there is much in Forje that reminds me of the way Aymeric moves as my enforcer. My Father always told me that an Alpha's Teeth is obvious from the way he moves in a fight.

Of course, when Neera comes out of the house all huffy and exasperated that the boys are fighting yet again, I pretend that I was just about to break up the fight. Knowing me better than that and not fooled one bit by my pseudo-anger at the boys, my little Howl just rolls her eyes at me and marches them back in the house so she can clean them up.

Sometimes she won't look at me if one of the boys is a little bloodier than she likes, and I'll shift and whine at her, nudging her with my snout. Then, if I'm still being ignored, my wolf will roll onto his back and give her his belly, his tongue hanging out of his mouth in such a ridiculous way that Neera immediately caves and scratches his belly. At that point, I shift back, sending the boys outside to be watched by their guards while Neera and I go to the bedroom to read books.

When my parents pulled this shit and disappeared into their bedroom, I had to imagine them reading books for my own sanity, but since this is my Howl, the truth is I take her in the bedroom and fuck her six ways to Sunday.

"You know I love you?" I always said when I could finally find my words again.

Her little hand would cup my face. "It's right there in your eyes, Night, every time I look," she always said back. Then she'd put her lips against my ear and whisper how much she loved me...and life would feel so full and complete, I never needed anything more.

She was right, though, and my feelings for her were right there in my eyes, for her to see, for everyone to see, because my pack members always commented on how besotted I acted with my Howl, how I ran to her like a little boy with his first crush whenever she was around, how I always had to be touching her if she was within arms' reach...and if she wasn't, I would move until she was.

Their teasing didn't bother me. The relationship between an Alpha and his Howl was critical for a pack's well-being. Much as touching my hand soothed and settled pack members, the pack was also calmed by the affection I showed Neera and that she showed me. The years since Neera and I had Taken the Blood had been good ones for Aibek pack. In the bleak years following the war, when our pack had suffered so many losses, we'd been a bit lost. I had been a young Alpha, prepared by my father...yet wholly unprepared for assuming the mantle of Alpha at such a young age.

Since Neera had become my Howl, I felt my pack members settling into a more peaceful existence. One night, the Forces favored me with a dream that I was given permission to share with Néron. It was the same dream in which I learned Neera was carrying my pup and what his name would be.

I'd opened my eyes and found myself outside, bathed in the light of a full moon, and my parents, whole and healthy, were together, holding hands as they always had, looking at me. Both of them were smiling, their faces happy.

"You've done well, son," my father, my Alpha, had said to me. "You and your Howl are strong and good together. The pup Neera's carrying, Darius, will one day lead Aibek pack, the strongest pack in the land."

Father's practical message, pack-focused, was exactly what I'd expect from the man who taught me to be Alpha and the responsibilities it carried. Lead the pack. Take care of the pack. Prepare the next generation to lead the pack. And most of all, love your family so well that your happiness upholds the pack.

But my mother's message was as she had been. Sensitive. Loving. Understanding.

"Let it go, Night," she said softly, and I knew exactly what she was referring to. "Let that vision of us go and remember us like this. It's OK to be happy, son, and we'll be watching to make sure you are."

I woke from that dream and turned to look at Neera, slumbering peacefully beside me, her body holding a secret that would be very welcome news to her. I would wait until the next day, our wedding day, to tell her the news.

"Neera Karis, I can't wait to spend the rest of my life with you," I'd whispered to her.

Her eyes opened sleepily, a soft smile curving her lips.

"And why is that?" she'd asked me, her voice husky.

I trailed a fingertip down her soft cheek.

"Because I love you."

Such a simple statement of truth carried such weight that it seemed like it should take longer to say.

"Good to know," she said, her eyes lifting to meet mine. "Because I love you...Alpha."

Oh, yeah.

Sometimes, life was so good, you just had to howl your pleasure to the moon.

So we did.